COUP DE PIERRE
A Murder Mystery in 1850s Paris

Paul Bristow

GW00302098

Chapter One
Monday 2 June 1851 - London - Bethnal Green Cut

Although the offices of Luker and Ledouin, Investigation Agents, lay near the heart of London, they were not easy to find for all that. A twenty-minute stroll was enough to cover the distance from the Bank of England in Threadneedle Street to Bishopsgate Station, but first-time visitors needed another ten minutes to walk the length of the railway terminus and then zigzag along the side streets to find 13 Bethnal Green Cut – one of the buildings thrown up over the decade since the Station opened, to accommodate a mixture of transportation and forwarding companies, and the associated froth of accountants and lawyers. There were half a dozen name-plates affixed to the front-door: Luker and Ledouin's was the smallest of these and ironically, since their offices were at the top of the building, it hung below the others.

Bethnal Green Cut, when it was not swaying to one side or the other, ran north from the Station. The façade of No. 13 looked west; but the visitor to Luker and Ledouin's had to climb three flights of stairs, and with each tread more of the daylight fell away, like rain dropping from gabardine. Without the candles that burned all the working day, the attic rooms would have been darker than the basement.

Octavius Luker was happy with the situation. "My clients don't wish to see me in the bright light of day", he often muttered, with a slight chuckle. With his habitual stoop, and his hair slicked down across a forehead that overhung a pinched and squinting face, there was certainly little about him to be admired, though it was themselves that his clients preferred to conceal.

His visitor that afternoon was no different. Luker heard the huffing and puffing of his ascent some little while before the bulky figure stepped into his office. A man old enough to be Luker's father, draped in a coat of the best quality, he paused to draw breath, and then leaned over the desk where the Investigation Agent sat. "Are you Luker?"

He got up, walked round the desk, and extended a hand. "Octavius Luker, at your service, Mr - ?"

The hand was not taken, and the name not given. "Is there somewhere that I can sit down and talk to you in private?"

Luker smiled inwardly. It was hard to imagine any greater privacy than was already afforded by this garret space hidden behind Bishopsgate Station. But he had learnt to anticipate this question. "Of course. May I invite you to step through into the inner office?" He opened a door behind where he had been seated. "I'll bring the candle with us."

Luker went first. The meagre illumination from the flame showed the visitor a room scarcely larger than a storage cupboard: against one wall there were indeed several piles of paper bundles tied up with ribbon. But two leather-cushioned chairs of surprisingly good quality had also been installed, on either side of a small pedestal table where Luker placed the candle.

The visitor sat down heavily in one of the chairs and ran his gaze rapidly over the room. "I see that you waste no money on the comforts of life." He looked at Luker. "Good!"

"If I tell you, sir, that much of my time is spent not in these offices but in the wider world, in pursuit of – investigations – you will understand that improving these rooms is not of great concern to me."

"Aye, that's all to the good." He coughed. "And these papers – do they relate to your investigations?"

"Indeed they do. However, rest assured that none of the matters recorded in these papers are of a confidential nature. Such affairs remain here -" he pointed a crooked finger at his head, "and are not committed to the written record."

"Aye, aye, all to the good." There was a silence.

"May I ask, sir, whether our firm has been recommended to you?"

"No. I saw mention of it in my newspaper, in reference to one Septimus Luker."

Luker gave his pinched smile. "Ah, my brother. Yes, he was much in the public eye two years back. The case of the Moonstone, was it not?"

"Aye, that it was. Did you follow it?"

"No more than any of my fellow men, sir. Septimus Luker is indeed my brother, but since we left our parents' house I have had few dealings with him." Luker looked more closely at his visitor. "May I ask whether you have some special interest in the case?"

"You may." There was a pause. "I have. And it is to serve that interest that I am here today." Luker was accustomed to the hesitations of his clients. He allowed them to set their own pace in asking for his services. "There were several individuals who played a part in the events which took place then, and which culminated two years ago in the death of Mr Godfrey Ablewhite." The older man stopped, and breathed deeply. When he spoke again, there was a new agitation in his voice. "But the individual – the individual who bears most of the blame for the tragedy is one Franklin Blake!" He fell silent, but his face was flushed crimson.

"I think I recall the details now. Mr Blake has subsequently married Miss Verinder, I believe."

"Aye, he has. A fine match they make too!" The words flowed out on a wash of contempt. Luker noticed that the emotion in his visitor's voice was matched by the sudden redness which spread across his cheeks and up his brow to mottle his bald head. "Well, Luker, we come to the crux. I have reason, good reason which I shall not disclose to you, to withhold my goodwill from Mr Franklin Blake. I opine that he is a man of little consistency and no honour. I wish to strengthen my opinion by discovering proofs of his past wrong-doing. And I hope that you are the man to assist me in this endeavour."

Luker gripped his pale hands together. "I should be honoured to assist you, sir. But first -"

"You wish to know what recompense you will receive?" Luker had intended to ask about the visitor's relationship with Blake, but kept his silence. The older man fetched something from a pocket inside his coat. "I propose a monthly retainer of ten pounds, payable at the start of each month, and beginning now." He put ten pounds on the little table. It was more than enough.

"I readily accept the commission, Mr -"

"There is no need for you to know my name. I shall visit your offices on the first Monday of each month to learn what you discover." He reached inside his coat again and placed a sheet of paper on the table. "I am providing you with the addresses of the residences in London and Yorkshire of Mr Blake and his family." The visitor stood up, then abruptly asked: "Who is Ledouin?"

Luker was not surprised by the question. "One moment, sir. I shall introduce him to you." He stepped out of the room. A minute later the door opened again, and in stepped a figure who stood two or three inches taller than Luker. "*Mes compliments*," the man said. "Olivier Ledouin." An upright fringe of hair floated around his temples, as he held his head back, smiling broadly. He wore a long, open coat, and presented a gloved hand bearing a card with his name. "I am delighted to make your acquaintance."

The voice was high-pitched, and marked by a distinct French accent, but the visitor caught some familiar tones in it: and now he saw beyond the the aura of foreignness that had been wrapped around Ledouin as he entered. "Luker?"

Ledouin gave an expansive bow – and, as he resumed his normal posture, the disguise fell away and Octavius Luker re-appeared, hunched, furtive, and thoroughly English. "As you see, sir. Ledouin is none other than Luker. But two heads are better than one on a company name-plate – and I have found that several of my clients have been pleased to avail themselves of my mastery of the French tongue." He took off his coat and gloves.

"Speak it well, do you?"

Luker's hands twisted against each other. "Tolerably well, sir."

The visitor grunted. "I won't ask you how you came by that ability. But it may serve in the work that I want you to perform. And now, good day to you!"

Luker bustled out ahead, bearing the candle aloft. No more words passed between them as the visitor left the offices and lumbered heavily down the stairs. As he heard the street door open and close, Luker followed, locking his office behind him and scampering confidently down to the ground floor. "I'll take your money, sir, and keep your secrets, but I mean to find out just who you are." He opened the street door slowly. There was no-one outside. Luker made silent haste southwards along the Cut, and was rewarded for his zeal by the sight of his visitor steering his way past the Station in the direction of the City. The man walked steadily and confidently, without a backward glance. "And why should you look over your shoulder, sir?" Luker thought. "No-one has ever suspected you of wrong-doing. No-one would ever shadow your steps to catch you out – no-one but Octavius Luker." A smile played on his pinched face. "God bless the solid citizens of London, who have the trick of handing me money without turning their eyes on my person. How many times have they held their names back from me, and how many times have I followed them to their mansions or their business chambers as easily as if they had given me their own visiting cards." He patted the pocket in which he was carrying the ten pounds just received. "God bless them indeed. May their hands be as open as their eyes are closed!"

The pursuit did not last long. After fifteen minutes, Luker's client arrived at the steps of one of the finance-houses that nestled against the skirts of the Old Lady of Threadneedle Street. Without a moment's hesitation, he climbed the steps, received the greeting of the porter at the main door, and went straight inside. Luker bided his time, standing in the shadows opposite the entrance. When an hour had passed and his client had not re-emerged, Luker took it as given that the man had his office there. It would prove easy enough to establish his identity now. He made his way back to Bethnal Green Cut, feeling pleased with his afternoon's work.

In the weeks that followed, the investigation agent did justice to the payment which he had received. It so happened that Franklin Blake and his wife, the former Miss Rachel Verinder, were spending the summer at their London house, in Montagu Square, and this meant that the house was also full of cooks, maids and footmen. It was one of the latter that Luker drew into closer acquaintance.

He watched George Harrowgill for several days. After establishing that he favoured the "Bulldog" tavern which lay half-way between his master's house and the markets of Covent Garden, he drank with him on successive days until young George (who had not yet reached his third decade) was convinced that his new companion was one of his oldest friends. Finally, George told Luker that he had entered Mr Blake's service only a year before, but had often heard the other servants talk about the drama of the diamond – and that he had recently seen a great pile of papers on Mr Blake's desk of which his master had said: "Whatever you do, George, don't disturb these writings. They are the true record of my family's entanglement with the Moonstone, and I have brought them together through no little effort. Whatever befalls our memories in years to come, here we have the truth of this strange family story."

Luker knew that pulling suddenly on the line risked losing the catch, but here was the fish he needed to land. He wheedled out of George that, though the papers were his master's prize possession, they were heaped up carelessly on his desk, and risked collapse if the windows were opened and a breeze blew in. Luker got the landlord to re-fill George's tankard: then he told him that he knew a book-binder - Master Nathaniel Finch, of Globe Town - who could stitch papers together and give them a good solid cover, at a good price: why didn't George win his master's favour by offering to get the family record safely tied and bound?

Several days passed before the agent and the footman met again in the "Bulldog". The bait had been taken. George was as pleased as Punch that Mr Blake had slapped him heartily on the back and sent him off to the book-binders there and then.

This was no news to Luker. He had worked with Nathaniel Finch in the past; and the night before his latest visit to George's tavern, Luker had sat in Finch's workshop and, by the light of three candles, read the account of the Moonstone from start to finish. Franklin Blake's papers were still with Finch; but every detail that could assist him was firmly imprinted in Luker's mind. He knew everything that Blake had done during the year that had passed between the loss of the Moonstone in Yorkshire and its re-appearance in London (through the agency of Septimus Luker); but more importantly, he had discovered promising information about Blake's deeds, and misdeeds, in the youthful years he had passed on the continent of Europe.

George had deserved the ale that Luker had bought him; the older man wished him well as he explained that a change in his work made it unlikely that he would find his way to the "Bulldog" again.

***

Monday 7 July 1851 - London - Bethnal Green Cut

Luker was ready for the next visit by the client whom he thought of as Mr Blake-Hater (though he now knew his real name). On the first Monday of the month, he sat at his desk in the outer office and ran over in his mind what he had discovered, as he waited for the heavy footfalls on the stairs. Shortly after two o'clock he heard them; and, when Mr Blake-Hater appeared in the doorway, still panting from the effort of the climb, Luker jumped up and ushered him through to the private chamber.

There was silence for a few moments as the visitor got his breath back. Then: "Well, Luker, what have you to tell me?"

"A good deal, sir, and much that bears upon your purpose." He gave an account of his dealings with the young footman, and of the insights that he had gained from reading the Moonstone papers. His visitor had overcome any fatigue, and sat forward on his chair to hear every detail. "Having read the papers from first to last, sir, I beg to suggest that they contain two pointers, two way-markers if you will, that could lead to the proofs of character of which you spoke before.

"The steward to the Verinder household in Yorkshire, one Gabriel Betteredge, writes about the years which Mr Blake spent in France, Germany and Italy before his return to England some three years ago. Betteredge says in particular that his intention to return was twice thwarted by a woman, whose name unfortunately is not given in the papers. This is the first pointer.

"I found the second and, I believe, more fruitful signpost in Mr Blake's own contribution to the papers. On his return to England, he stayed for several weeks at the Verinder household, and he has set down that, towards the end of his stay there, a French lawyer came to Yorkshire to seek payment of a debt that the young man had incurred in the form of a loan from the keeper of a restaurant in Paris. Mr Blake writes that Lady Julia Verinder herself intervened, to pay off the debt and to ensure that the lawyer went back to his native land without further alarm. In Mr Blake's own words, which I retain clearly in my mind, without her Ladyship's intervention his position might have become a very disgraceful one." Luker paused.

"He wrote that, did he? Well, I wish no harm to the memory of Lady Verinder, but," and the visitor shook his head as he spoke, "she acted imprudently to shield the blackguard from the consequences of his own wrong-doing. You have done well, Luker. But names? Are there names given?"

"I regret not, sir. But I have a proposal to make." He paused.

"Aye? Out with it, then."

"Mr Blake writes that, when he found it impossible to repay the loan in Paris, he sent the keeper a bill. The lawyer who travelled from France to Yorkshire must have carried that bill with him, and left it with the late Lady Verinder when the debt was settled. Is it not likely that the bill still remains among her Ladyship's papers which the family may have retained since her demise?"

"Aye, likely enough. But how would you propose that the bill be brought to light?"

"I have given some thought to that question. I could seek the assistance of young Mr Harrowgill, but on balance I think that inadvisable. It is to be assumed that the late Lady Verinder's papers have been kept in the house in Yorkshire, where she spent most of her time, and for so long as Mr and Mrs Blake stay in London, Mr Harrowgill will be here with them. And in any case I cannot presume too much upon the young man's compliance – he might himself question the reason for burrowing into such family papers."

"I follow you on that, Luker. But how do you answer these difficulties?"

Luker gave his visitor a crooked smile. "I have an answer sir, but, with your leave, I had best keep it to myself. Rest assured, I shall use a method which has reliably delivered results in the past."

The other man moved on his chair. "Make what shift you can, Luker. I have taken a long spoon, and am ready to sup with it. So much for the second of what you call the pointers. But what of the first? What of this foreign Jezebel who kept Blake away from England?"

"I cannot expect to discover her name in the family papers, sir, or indeed anywhere in this country. But experience tells me that, where young men have run up debts in Parisian hostelries, women are habitually implicated. If I can discover the name of the Frenchy restaurant-keeper who stood credit to Mr Blake, then we may look to him to guide us to the *mademoiselle* in question."

"You know the world, Luker." There was a nuance of admiration in the visitor's voice. "And I don't doubt that you know Paris also – or your associate, Ledouin, does. Do you have in mind to take your investigation to France as well?"

"It may become necessary, sir, though I know citizens of that country who may assist me."

"Well, I have my long spoon, and I shall evidently have to use it." He took money from his coat pocket. "Here is your next payment. I trust that your plans will be further ahead when we meet in a month's time." The interview was at an end. Luker lit the way out, and listened as Mr Blake-Hater went down the stairs and out into the Cut. Luker sat down again, running his thin fingers to and fro over the ten pounds on his desk, and thinking.

***

Friday 18 July 1851 - Yorkshire

It was some two weeks later that his thoughts came to fruition. The Blakes were in London for some months, and the house in Yorkshire had been closed up and placed under covers. But Luker knew, both from reading the Moonstone papers and from George Harrowgill's indiscretions, that Gabriel Betteredge, the steward, stayed in Yorkshire with the two guard-dogs, as well as the gardener, the cook and one of the house-maids. Four pairs of eyes – or six, if the dogs were counted in, as they should be – would easily spot any stranger who approached the house in an innocent way.

No, stealth and guile were required. Silas Snagge was not acknowledged on Luker and Ledouin's name-plate, but he had been a close associate of Octavius Luker for as long as he had been an investigation agent. Most people made took a horizontal course through life, along paving-stones and through doorways: Snagge's progress was more often vertical, up and down drain-pipes, and then through windows forced open against their will; for all that he stood no taller than a twelve-year-old boy, he was the best climber-and-cracker in the metropolis. In meetings seen by no-one else, Luker had learnt more from Snagge about the exteriors of houses in and around London than was known even to their owners, and had received from him documents brought back as keepsakes of his nocturnal expeditions which allowed Luker to guide several of his cases to a speedy conclusion.

Snagge was the answer that Luker had withheld from Mr Blake-Hater. The investigation agent and his vertical man travelled to Yorkshire together. In Frizinghall, Luker stayed at the hotel while Snagge found himself a billet at an edge-of-town tavern. As night fell, they joined forces and walked across to the grounds of the old Verinder house. The moon was full, as they had foreseen. Snagge took from his sack the cuts of meat that he had bought at the butcher's in town. Luker had the bottle of laudanum. They drenched the meat with the sedative and reached over the wall to drop it beyond. Their wait lasted little more than fifteen minutes. They heard the sounds of the dogs as they padded up to the meat, sniffed and ate it greedily. Five minutes more, and they heard the thud of canine bodies against the ground. Luker nodded to Snagge, who was over the wall, across the grounds and up the side of the house with all the speed he could muster.

Luker settled down, in patience. He had given Snagge all the intelligence about the house that he had acquired, including his knowledge that the late Lady Verinder's rooms had been on the first floor, at the western end. Beyond that, however, success depended on the vertical man's initiative: Snagge had to ensure that he could move inside the house without being detected; Snagge had to locate the papers of the deceased chatelaine; and Snagge had to sift from them the key document, the bill signed by Mr Blake in favour of the Parisian restaurant-keeper. But Luker felt confident: "Snagge always gets the swag", he told himself; and promising him a guinea for a job well done made the outcome even more certain.

Half an hour passed. "Snagge gets the swag", Luker reminded himself. When an hour had elapsed, the agent felt a first pang of concern. Five or so minutes to get into the house, and five more to find the room. Surely forty-five must be long enough to search through her Ladyship's papers, even using the moon-light to read. Luker stood up to look over the wall, and at that moment Snagge slipped down beside him. The grin on his face told all. He handed Luker a folded letter.

"Thank you. Was it difficult?" Snagge shook his head. "And you weren't seen?"

Snagge's grin broadened further. "Come off it, Mr Luker."

"And you took nothing for yourself?"

"You know me - honest as the day is long."

Luker did not press the issue, but put a guinea in Snagge's hand. "Until the next time, Silas."

"Always a pleasure, Mr Luker." They made their way back to Frizinghall, Snagge running ahead of the agent. They had no need to stay together now, and no wish to be seen in each other's company. And within another hour or so, the dogs could be expected to shake off the effects of the sedative and start sniffing around the grounds again.

Luker had looked at the letter as soon as Snagge gave it to him. Once he was back in his hotel room, he studied it more carefully. Written in what he recognised as Franklin Blake's hand, it was dated 1847, and confirmed a debt of 1,000 French francs owed for a loan made to Blake by M. Jean-Marie Ricord, proprietor of the *Auberge des Dunes*, Rue de Calais, Paris.

"One thousand francs," mused Luker. "Nigh on fifty pounds. What use did you make of that money, Mr Blake?" He folded the letter up again, and hid it inside his coat. "They say that money makes money. Well, this bill of yours will help Mr Blake-Hater open his wallet to me again." With such thoughts in his head, Luker slept soundly that night, and headed back to London early the next morning, separately from Snagge.

***

Monday 4 August 1851 - London - Bethnal Green Cut

Little more than a fortnight later, Luker sat again in his private office with his portly client in the chair opposite. His visitor was scrutinising the bill that had travelled down from Yorkshire in the agent's pocket. "One thousand francs." He looked more closely at the writing. "Well, I doubt that Monsieur Ricord ever loaned money to a less reliable customer than Mr Franklin Blake. And poor Lady Verinder had to empty her own purse to drag Mr Blake's chestnuts out of the fire. It should have been a warning to her!"

"I fear that her Ladyship's better judgement must have been trumped by the wishes of Miss Verinder."

"Aye, a headstrong young woman, if ever there was one." He folded the letter up, then paused as he seemed about to put it into his own pocket. "You have not said how this bill came into your possession, Luker, and I desire you not to tell me. On balance, however, I think it better to leave the document in your care. It would not be seemly if I were found to have acquired it." He set it down on the table. "I trust that you can stow it somewhere safe."

"You may rely on me for that, sir."

"You have done well to ferret out this information, Luker. Now we know where Mr Franklin Blake squandered his time and wealth when he was in Paris. How do you propose to take the investigation further? Will you now journey to the French capital?"

Luker took a second or two before answering, and kept his gaze on his interlocked, writhing hands. "I have given thought to the question, sir, and I may well wish to travel to Paris myself, as you admit. However, as good fortune would have it, there are natives of that city who are currently amongst us, here in London, and as my next step I have in mind to test their knowledge."

"Currently here in London, you say?"

"Indeed sir. In London, and drawn to the Great Exhibition in the Crystal Palace. A magnificent presentation of all that our country has achieved in manufacture and commerce. And a spectacle that has attracted not only our fellow countrymen, but also visitors from the nations of Europe, and the United States."

"By that you mean Parisians who are familiar with the type of bawdy-house frequented by Mr Franklin Blake?"

"*Tout le monde de Paris*, if you will pardon my French – high and low. You may not know this, sir," and Luker lowered his voice, as though exchanging a confidence, "but the Metropolitan Police has invited its counterpart forces in France, Germany and America to send several of their own officers to London to assist in the work of policing the Great Exhibition, to intercept any compatriot pickpockets, cutpurses or other delinquents who have travelled here to ply their ignoble trade."

"Has it indeed? Aye, well, if you put the family silver in the parlour and let the world walk in, what can you expect?" He put money on the table. "Here's twenty pounds, Luker. Circumstances will not allow me to call here in September, but I shall be back the following month. Make your inquiries. Dig me out Mr Franklin Blake's French fancy, and you will not find me ungrateful!"

Luker took time over the next stage of his investigation. He had little doubt that Mr Blake-Hater would cover the cost of as many journeys to Paris as Luker might find needful, but he wanted first to prepare the ground.

Several times during the summer he joined the crowds flocking to the great Palace in Hyde Park; and, by moving constantly and eavesdropping on the chatter around him, he overheard numerous snippets of French and, carefully and covertly, observed the individuals who were speaking it, and took a view of their place in society.

There were fewer from the lower echelons, but his instinct was sound. Before the heat of the summer faded, Luker had conducted several conversations with one resident of Paris, temporarily transplanted to London, who knew the Rue de Calais and had drunk in the *Auberge des Dunes*. He shared his knowledge with the investigation agent. Learning that his French informant would be staying in London until the Exhibition ended, Luker held open the possibility that he might consult him again after his own journey to Paris.

***

Wednesday 3 September 1851 - Paris - Rue de Calais

And in early September, Olivier Ledouin (newly arrived from England) visited the tavern in the Rue de Calais. It seemed to him a shabby part of the city, no better than the cramped and dirty streets of Bethnal Green that spilled out from the Cut. But the *Auberge des Dunes* came as a surprise: it was no Grand Hotel, but the bar-room was light, with plenty of candles when night fell, and half a dozen tables where food was being consumed alongside wine and beer. Jean-Marie Ricord, the tavern-keeper, kept his own counsel: as he served

Ledouin, he offered him the briefest of smiles even as his eyes looked him over, making the type of assessment that Ledouin himself habitually performed.

Without his preparatory work in London, Ledouin might have learnt no more from Ricord than the cost of the meal and wine that he consumed. But his interlocutor at the Great Exhibition had authorised mention of his name to the tavern-keeper; and it acted as a pass-word to get Ledouin past the man's defences.

After glancing round the bar to make sure that he was not needed elsewhere, Ricord sat down at the agent's table. "Tell me who you are again."

"Olivier Ledouin."

"A French name. But you say you live in England."

"I work in London as an investigation agent." He handed him a card.

The Frenchman glanced at it, then used it to pick his teeth. "Is that why you're here now?"

"I won't waste your time, Monsieur Ricord. I have been retained by a client in London to discover evidence of dishonourable conduct by another citizen of England. It is a family matter, but I am aware that the subject of my investigation is known to you." He saw a first spark of understanding in Ricord's eyes. "If I say that this subject received a loan from you some four years ago which he failed to repay on the due date, would that prompt any recollection?"

"Franklin Blake!" Ledouin nodded. Ricord leaned in close and hissed: "That man brought me to the edge of ruin. If you know that, what more evidence do you need?"

Ledouin had not yet poured wine from the bottle on his table. He did so now, and gave the glass to the tavern-keeper. "Drink this, and I shall explain." Ricord paused, then drank. "Mr Blake's actions caused you difficulties. But, unprincipled though the man may be, I cannot believe that he sought so large an advance of money from you and failed to re-pay it with the sole aim of causing you distress, Monsieur Ricord. I know that he was no stranger to female company during his travelling years. I believe that he took money from you to put it into the hands of a woman, as payment for services rendered or pending. My investigation so far has brought me to your tavern, and to you. I hope that you can guide me further, to find the woman with whom Mr Blake dishonoured himself."

Ricord had drained the glass and now re-filled it. "If you find this woman, what then?"

"Then I shall speak to her, and hear what she has to say about Mr Blake, and present my account to my client in London."

"And then?"

"That is a matter for my client. But I may fairly say that his detestation of Mr Blake is in no way inferior to yours, Monsieur Ricord. Unless I am mistaken, he intends to use the information that I provide as a cutting blade which he will cause to fall on the neck of Mr Blake."

The tavern-keeper raised the glass in approval and drank deeply. "There was a woman. Blake brought her here many times. The last time, they quarrelled, and left – she ran first, and he ran after her. The next day Blake got one thousand francs from me. I never saw her again, and Blake stayed away, until first he defaulted on the loan and then he hurried back to England."

"A sorry tale, Monsieur Ricord. Who was this woman?"

Ricord snorted. "She styles herself Suzanne Pâquerette. Go to the Théâtre Parisien, behind the Palais Royal. You'll find her there." He drained the glass again. "Blake may have closed his ears to her voice, but many other men are still happy to listen to it." He stood up and left him.

Ledouin finished his meal on his own, and went out into the evening. He had taken a cab from his hotel in the heart of Paris to the Rue de Calais, but there was little prospect of finding one to convey him back. He was no stranger to the city, though, and knew how to find the Palais Royal. His feet got him to the theatre some thirty minutes later. He paid to be admitted, and joined the crowd inside. A succession of painted and preened women appeared on the stage, singing, dancing and bathing in the enthusiasm of the male spectators. When the performance ended, Ledouin followed

25

several other men back-stage. One of them told him that La Pâquerette had trilled two or three songs at the start of the evening: he would point her out to Ledouin if he saw her behind the scenes. But he did not.

It was from the theatre manager that Ledouin learnt that Suzanne Pâquerette had already left the theatre, with an admirer. Ledouin briefly explained why he wanted to talk to her. The manager undertook to tell her, and to encourage her to send a message to Ledouin at his lodgings, if she was content to meet him.

Ledouin stayed in his hotel all the next day, sitting on one of the two chairs in the reception area. He had heard nothing by the time evening fell. He had all but resolved to force the issue by returning to the theatre when the hotel door opened and a grey-haired woman, wrapped in a long cape, came in and asked for Monsieur Ledouin. He jumped to his feet and made his introduction.

"I am Madame Armandine Sauvigny, *monsieur*." She had a pleasant voice, but it lacked force, as though worn down by the rigours of life. Her face was kindly, but pale and lined. "I am a cousin of Suzanne, and companion to her. I am here on her behalf." Ledouin gestured towards the chairs. The woman moved wearily, and sat down slowly, as though it cost her considerable effort to do so. "You came to the theatre last night to talk to her. I have come in her place – Suzanne has had to leave Paris suddenly."

"She has left Paris?" Ledouin echoed.

"Her home, and mine, is in Provence. This morning we received word that Suzanne's mother is ill, and she has travelled south to see her. She may be away from the city for some time."

"How unfortunate. I am sorry for Mademoiselle Pâquerette and her mother – and I am sorry too if I miss the opportunity to speak to her before I return to England."

"When will that be?"

"In the circumstances, Madame Sauvigny, I may well depart tomorrow."

The woman considered this information for a few seconds. "You should understand, *monsieur*, that I have Suzanne's complete confidence. She sent me here not simply to offer you her apologies, but also to act in her name."

Ledouin's eyes brightened. "Then perhaps you will allow me to set out the reasons why I have travelled to Paris now, and why I sought an interview with Mademoiselle Pâquerette." He gave her the same account as he had presented to the tavern-keeper the previous evening. Armandine Sauvigny was attentive and, though she did not interrupt him, he thought that he noticed a flicker in her eyes, a nervous movement, when he mentioned Franklin Blake. "And so I had hoped, in speaking to Mademoiselle Pâquerette, and without wishing to cause her any embarrassment, to learn more about her acquaintanceship with Mr Blake – and about any publishable act by that gentleman which might be held up as proof of a dishonourable character."

Several seconds passed during which the woman was lost in thought. Then she turned her gaze on Ledouin, and her voice strengthened: "My cousin would not deny her association with that 'gentleman', at the time that you describe. She would not deny that she took pleasure in his company – as he appeared to do in hers." She paused. "She could undoubtedly say much that would discredit him." Her tone softened again. "But tell me, *monsieur*, why do you think she would choose to do so?"

"Forgive me if I talk of delicate matters, *madame*, but I know that your cousin and the gentleman fell out in public only a short time before the gentleman left this city to return to England. I cannot imagine that your cousin has retained a fond memory of their association."

"You may be right."

"And – I admit that this is particularly delicate – I know also that the gentleman took on a considerable loan after this quarrel – perhaps to offer your cousin monetary compensation for a failing in sentiment."

Ledouin was taken aback by the intensity with which the woman had fixed her eyes on his face. She lowered them again. "He did offer her money – and she took it. It was little enough for what she gave him. It was no compensation for her suffering. My cousin has had to live with that suffering for the last four years." The flow of words stopped, while Armandine Sauvigny reflected on her memories, and Ledouin digested what he had been told. Then she spoke again.

"I understand the purpose of your investigation, *monsieur*. Be assured that I shall share my understanding with Suzanne. You now know of her association with Franklin Blake, and you know something of the circumstances in which they parted. But you have only part of the picture. I cannot tell you more today. You must allow time for Suzanne to consider what you have told me, and to decide whether she wishes to help you further."

Ledouin nodded his agreement. "In that case, *madame*, I shall give you my card. I would ask that you, or your cousin, are good enough to write to me in London once that decision has been made."

The woman took the card and made sure of it in the purse which she carried. She stood up. "Goodbye, *monsieur*."

Ledouin went to hold the door open. "Goodbye, *madame*. Thank you."

She left without saying more. Ledouin watched as she walked awkwardly along the street; other pedestrians pushed past at twice her pace; but finally she disappeared around a corner. He stood in the doorway a little while longer, then came back into the hotel. "That may have been Armandine Sauvigny," he said to himself, "or it may have been Suzanne Pâquerette herself, acting the part." There was no more to be done. The following day saw him travel back to London.

***

October 1851 - London - Bethnal Green Cut

Luker had much to tell his client when the man returned to his offices on the first Monday of the following month. His account could not however include the decision of Suzanne Pâquerette, since she had not yet written to him. But Mr Blake-Hater was pleased by what he heard, so pleased that he again left double the normal payment, to cover the agent's out-of-pocket expenses while in Paris.

The Great Exhibition finished in the second week of October. Still without a letter from Paris, Luker made his way back there to talk to his contact again. The Frenchman listened carefully to what Luker told him about his meetings with Ricord, and Madame Sauvigny. At the Englishman's suggestion, he agreed to correspond with him after his own return to his native city, in case Luker needed any further help – "which I shall of course remunerate", Luker stressed.

And then, one late October afternoon, a letter was brought to Luker's offices. The agent fancied that, even though it had travelled over land and across the Channel, there was still a fragrance, a sweet scent, that clung to the envelope, and to the sheet of paper inside. It was dated the previous week, and sent from the French capital.

"Monsieur Ledouin - My cousin has communicated to me the details of her interview with you. I have reflected upon the wishes which you expressed to her.
My response is simple. I am happy to assist in your proposal, but on these conditions.
The 'gentleman' must come to Paris again. I must be able to see him again. His dishonour will follow. If you accept these conditions and choose to proceed, you can write to me at the Théâtre Parisien. With discretion -
Suzanne Pâquerette"

Luker read the letter several times, then held it under his nose as he considered its implications. He had completed his investigation; the blade had been hauled up above Franklin Blake's head; his next meeting with his client would determine whether, and when, that blade would fall.

Chapter Two
Wednesday 8 September 1852 - Paris

Lucien de Boizillac waited in the shadows outside the Théâtre Parisien. Night had fallen on the city two hours before, while over-fed and ageing men had jostled with younger – or at least, younger-looking – women inside the concert-hall, laughing and shouting as the lights, the music and the alcohol released their high spirits.

Boizillac had mixed feelings about the theatre. He didn't begrudge the concert-goers their evening of pleasure: in recent years, Paris had seen enough hardship, enough clashes between government and people in the days of blood when insurrection was suppressed, to allow a republic to succeed a monarchy, and an emergent emperor to replace a republic. If wine, women and song helped his fellow citizens to forget these griefs, it caused him no resentment. But, for all that his hat, coat and gloves could have been the dress of a Parisian dandy, it was not a pleasure that he could enjoy any more. Drinking in a theatre would not ease his mind of the knowledge he had gained during the last year, in his work for the Prefecture of Police.

When Louis-Napoléon, nephew of the great Emperor, staged the *coup d'état* in December 1851, most of

France hailed the return of the Bonaparte dynasty, and looked forward to the inevitable return of imperial rule. Boizillac, born five years after Waterloo, had grown up in awe of France's achievements under Napoléon Bonaparte. But his faith in the old imperial family was shattered by what he had seen of the backstage manipulation of events. His success in investigating a series of murders in the weeks before the *coup* had served only to demonstrate the truth that crime committed by the powerful went unpunished; and that those who controlled the state could always find ways to block the efforts of individuals who refused to accept that truth.

He had forced himself to swallow the bitter pill, and to heed the warning to give up his investigation or see the consequences visited upon those closest to him. It was a warning that had been delivered by the Duc de Morny, then Minister of the Interior, and half-brother to Louis-Napoléon. When Morny met Boizillac, he revealed that the Comte de Flahaut, who had fathered Morny with Louis-Napoléon's mother, had enjoyed a later liaison with Lucien's own mother. Morny and Boizillac were half-brothers too.

But it was not these unsuspected ties that led him to bow his head to the warning. It was the threat to Laure Cerise, the young woman who mattered most to him, and to her family. And it was because of Laure that Boizillac now stood in the shadows. Laure was an actress, and for the last few months she had been taken on by the Théâtre Parisien. When he was able to, Lucien walked her home when she left the theatre.

The evening wore on. It was often like this: even when the show ended, Laure and the other actresses had to endure the attentions of the wealthier theatre-goers who assumed the right to swarm through the backstage areas and seek to impress the young women with their money and their overbearing manners. None of this troubled Boizillac: he was sure of his companion. And the last year had accustomed him more generally to the art of waiting.

After the *coup*, Paris seemed at ease with the new rulers of France, keen to enjoy the glory and prosperity that Louis-Napoléon and his financier friends promised. But, like the Seine that flowed through it, the city had its backwaters and side-channels where murkier currents ran. The radicals who de-throned Louis-Philippe in 1848 and put a new republic in his place had not all disappeared only three or four years later. Some of them turned in the wind and gave their support to the new regime, but there were many others for whom 2 December 1851 with its *coup* was a day of shame, which they could not accept.

In the months that followed, the new Government made great efforts to track down those who still resisted. Summary justice was dispensed to those found guilty of conspiring against the new regime: if not executed, they were sent overseas to France's penal colonies in the Americas. Boizillac was one of the police agents deployed in this extended man-hunt, a game of cat-and-mouse which required him to bide his time in many of the city's dark places until his prey could be flushed out into the light.

It was not a game he would have chosen to play. He had joined the Paris police to use his skills, acquired in military service, against the robbers and cutthroats who infested the city's back-streets – not hunt down political agitators. He might not share their views, but nor did he believe that being anti-Bonapartist was a crime that deserved the punishment that Morny and his agents meted out.

Still, there were circumstances that went some way towards reconciling him to this questionable role. The threat made clear to him by Morny was directed at Laure's older brother, Marc Carreleur, arrested on the day of the *coup* because of his membership of a secret society which worked against France's domination of Algeria. Boizillac bowed his head to the new government, and Carreleur was allowed to live. It was only some months later, in the spring of 1852, that he discovered that Carreleur had turned his coat completely, and that, with the blessing of Persigny, Morny's successor as Interior Minister, he had been let out of custody after undertaking to act as an informant on his former co-conspirators. Carreleur's traitorous work was known only to a handful of figures who ran the state – and to Lucien: it had been settled, without the police agent's knowledge, that Carreleur would report to him.

And Carreleur did his job effectively, so that Boizillac had brought about the arrest of twenty or more resisters as the year progressed. When other state enforcers swept these men up, it was likely that they would use their pistols first and deliver their captives to the graveyard rather than the prison. That was not Lucien's way; and, though he knew that the men that he took could expect nothing better than transportation to the colonies, he reckoned that, if they survived arrest, they could survive the subsequent ordeal as well.

A light rain started to fall. Boizillac pulled his hat down more closely on his head, and turned up the collar of his greatcoat. The late-night strollers moved more quickly along the streets. One of them suddenly turned towards him, pressed a folded sheet of paper into his hand, saying "Another one for the galleys", and passed on before any more could be said.

It was Carreleur: it was his preferred way of passing information on. He had not contacted Boizillac outside the theatre before: that generally happened when Lucien left his lodgings. There was not enough light to read the paper now, but the police agent knew that it would contain a name, a brief description of the man's age and build, and an address. He would go there tomorrow.

And only a minute or so later Laure appeared, saw Boizillac, and ran to him, as she always did, and planted a kiss on his cheek. He put his arm around her and they started to walk home. Laure knew nothing of his pact with Morny, or her brother's recruitment as an informant. She rarely saw Carreleur, and believed what he had told her in a letter, that he was busy working as a mason in the construction boom that was gathering pace in the city. Lucien could not tell her the truth, and did not want to. The burden that the secret placed on his heart was a small price to pay for protecting her from the grief that Carreleur's deportation, or death, would have caused.

He stayed with Laure that night, marvelling as always at the happiness which together they created for themselves, away from the struggles and petty victories of the rest of the world. He left her still sleeping as the city came to life again the next morning. He had a job to do.

***

Thursday 9 September 1852

"*Cotte, Jacques. 33. Short, powerful. 4 Passage de la Douane (Canal Saint-Martin).*" Boizillac looked again at the note he had been passed by Carreleur. He had never seen Cotte's name before: though they were the same age, he reflected, their paths had never crossed, until that day. He would need to organise the arrest.

For the last year Boizillac had worked with Daniel Delourcq, twenty years older than him and with a lifetime's experience of crime in Paris, gained on both sides of the law. Delourcq knew the city like the back of his hand. For all the contrast between their places in society and their education - or lack of it - the two of them quickly formed a partnership, even friendship, that had helped Lucien through the disillusionment of the *coup* and his meeting with Morny. Delourcq knew of all that had transpired, and was at Boizillac's side throughout the subsequent months of the man-hunt.

They met, as they usually did at the start of the day, in the *Chien Fou*, a tavern within spitting distance of the Prefecture of Police. Delourcq, with his battered, weather-worn face and clothes, looked like the other regulars who sat at tables with their first wine of the day. Boizillac, who still had the air of a young notable, with his greatcoat and gloves, was like a fish out of water; but, after months of drinking there with Delourcq, his presence was no longer remarkable.

"Another name for today," was all the younger man said as he sat down at Delourcq's table.

The other man grunted and drained his glass. "Can't be many left." He poured a second glass. "Drink up, captain. You won't get wine like this anywhere else." It was an old joke, but they both smiled. Delourcq pushed his plate across, for Boizillac to eat the dark bread and sausage that was often their breakfast. They allowed themselves a few minutes of sociability, then left for the Prefecture.

It took no more than an hour to make the usual arrangements. Boizillac and Delourcq would go on ahead to observe the neighbourhood where Cotte was hiding away: two *sergents de ville* would follow later, and link up with them at eleven. Exactly when, and how, the man was to be arrested would be decided by Boizillac on the spot.

The young captain and his partner made their way across the city on foot. The Canal St Martin was one of the main thoroughfares into Paris for boat-borne cargo: as it came within sight of the city's heart, it ran alongside the Place des Marais where the warehouses of the joint stock company, the Compagnie des Douanes, were ranged. Their long walls, made of solid stone, stretched shadows over the square and the streets behind.

Delourcq spat as they approached the canal. "Didn't like this place from the day it was built, twenty years ago." Boizillac waited for an explanation. "Made it too easy to get fancy goods into the city legally. Did nothing for my old trade."

"But I'm sure I've heard that some of the bonded goods managed to disappear on their way across the quay from the barge to the hall."

Delourcq gave a short laugh, and spat again. "Well, nothing's perfect, is it?"

The impression of order which the straight lines of the warehouse gave to the canalside was immediately dispelled by the jumble of older buildings and streets which Boizillac and Delourcq reached as they walked past the depot. "You know where this passage is?" the younger man asked.

"Follow me. But watch what you step in." They crossed the road that flanked the back of the warehouse: the cobbles were clogged with straw and manure that fell from the carts and horses which plied to and from the customs hall. A street led from the square to the Rue des Marais. Opposite them they saw the sagging outline of the Wauxhall ball-room; like an ageing *demi-mondaine*, daylight washed away the mystery and charm that radiated from it at night. On either side of it were dark alleyways, leading into an older Paris that had grown up long before the canal was driven into its heart. Delourcq stopped at the start of one of these alleyways. "Passage de la Douane" he explained. There was no name-plate: once again, Boizillac thanked his good fortune for being able to rely on Delourcq's knowledge of the city.

"Do you know where number 4 is?"

The older man spat. "I know this rat-run goes on for about as long as a speech by the Prefect, saving your presence. And I don't expect they hang the numbers on the doors. Not the sort of street where they welcome strangers." He paused; the two men looked at each other, and nodded at a shared thought. "If you stay here for the moment, captain, I'll do the reconnaissance. I'm less likely to be noticed." It was agreed.

Boizillac crossed back to the other side of the Rue des Marais. Ten minutes passed, then fifteen. Finally, Delourcq emerged from the gloom of the passage and rejoined him. "Number 4 is at the far end, on the right. Two upper storeys, front door a couple of steps down from the alleyway, painted black, door-knob in the shape of a bloody great mushroom." He paused. "No sign of life, except for a half-starved mongrel that cocked his leg against the door."

"And the passage gives on to another street down there?" Delourcq nodded. "In that case, we'll wait until the others arrive. We'll post one of them here, and the other one at the far end. Then you and I can invite ourselves into number 4, and see if Cotte is at home."

The two men had an hour or more to wait. Delourcq retraced his steps along the passage-way and worked round the connecting streets to remind himself of the area.   Then, with Boizillac's agreement, they took refuge in a local tavern for half an hour. Finally, after linking up with Dubost and Tenot, the *sergents*, they closed in on the targeted house.

The younger man strode up to the door with the mushroom handle and knocked loudly, using his gloved hand.   There was no response at first; then, at the muffled sound of footsteps from within, Boizillac looked at his companion; then silence again.   He hit the door once more, with greater force, and called out: "Cotte? We are from the Prefecture of Police. Give yourself up." Silence again.

"Time for me to knock?" Delourcq asked. Boizillac nodded, and stood to one side. The older man used all the strength in his legs to kick at the door. It flew open. Delourcq barged in, only to find Cotte in the shadows behind. The man held a thick wooden stake, half his height.   As Delourcq tumbled into the house, Cotte swung the stake against the incomer's legs and brought him crashing to the floor. He jumped over Delourcq and, even as Lucien moved forward into the house, Cotte charged straight at him, using the stake as a battering ram.   The police captain fell sideways, winded, as Cotte rushed into the alleyway, throwing down the stake, and running at full speed in the direction of the canal.

Boizillac gulped to get his breath back. "Delourcq?"

"Go after him," he shouted. He tried to raise himself from the floor, but slumped sideways. "He's done for one of my legs. Go and get him!"

The younger man raced along the passage. He heard a pistol shot, and then a shout of pain. Reaching the Rue des Marais, he could see Cotte running on, heading towards the Place des Marais, his left hand clamped over his right arm. "What happened?" he asked Dubost, who held the pistol. His lip had burst.

"I shot him once, but before I could fire again the bastard head-butted me."

Boizillac didn't stop. "Follow me!" He headed after Cotte; the man seemed to be slowing; he saw a red trail on the ground. The shot had done some damage.

The customs warehouses were in front of them. Cotte looked round, saw his pursuer, and found the strength to go faster, and hurry round the buildings towards the canal. "Give yourself up!" Boizillac shouted as he ran, closing the gap. "There's nowhere for you to go, Cotte."

And then the escaping man was at the side of the canal. He stopped. Boizillac was thirty or forty paces away from him. Then the pistol fired again; almost simultaneously, Boizillac saw Cotte plunge into the water. It was only a matter of seconds for him to run to the quayside, but though there were flecks of blood

42

visible on the murky surface below, the man himself was nowhere to be seen.

"Damn!" He turned to Dubost. "Keep an eye on the canal. He may drown, or he may haul himself out on one of the quays. Don't use your pistol again. If he survives, he'll be weak enough that you can take him without firing off any more bullets. I'll go back for the others."

But even as Boizillac made his way back to the Rue des Marais, he met up with Delourcq, limping along the street and leaning heavily on Tenot. "I'll support you," he said, and took Delourcq's right arm around his shoulder. "Cotte was hit by at least one shot in the arm, and fell into the canal. You," he called to Tenot "go on ahead and join in the search for him."

They watched him run on. "You think Cotte is fish-food now?" Delourcq asked, and grunted as his right foot twisted on the ground.

"I'll believe it when I see it. He was bleeding badly, but the man has the strength of an ox. What did he do to you?"

"I thought he'd broken my leg. But I'm pretty sure it's in the same lousy state as before, only I can't stand on it."

"Do you want to rest here?"

"No, if you can bear to drag me along, get me to the canal so we can see what's happened. I'll feel better if they've managed to grab the wretch!"

The two men struggled on. But Cotte had disappeared. The two *sergents* assured Boizillac that, between them, they had checked the canal itself for two hundred metres in either direction, both water and quayside: there was no sign of the man. Boizillac dismissed them.

Delourcq had perched himself on a mooring bollard, and was scanning the scene himself. "What do you think?" Boizillac asked.

The older man spat into the canal. "He may have bought it, and his body is trapped under one of these barges. In which case, the eels will get to him before we ever do. Or..." he paused.

"He may have been smarter than our friends, Dubost and Tenot, and hauled himself out of the canal without being seen?"

Delourcq nodded and spat again. "Like you said, captain, he has the strength. And the determination too, I guess. If it was only his arm that was hit, his legs could have saved him – unlike mine!" He grunted again.

"I'll make some inquiries in the streets around here. But first I'll get a cab for you. You'd better go home and deal with your injury. What will Françoise say?"

Delourcq laughed grimly. "What she always says. Anyone who does dirty business like us should expect to fall in the shit sometimes." The younger man grinned. "She's a good woman, but she's no friend of the police, even if she still sleeps with one. Begging your pardon, captain." A cab pulled up. The older man slumped into the back and rode home to the rooms that he and Françoise rented in a tenement block in the Rue de Reuilly.

Boizillac spent the next two hours checking with the bargemen and porters around the canal, with the *concierges* in the houses round about, and with the hawkers and street-dwellers who haunted the alleys that radiated out from the canal. No-one had seen Cotte; and though he thought that some of them would find it easier to walk on water than to tell the truth, he had to accept that, if the man had escaped, he was not going to find any trace of him that day. Perhaps he had perished in the canal, and his body would surface when one of the boats moved away. There was no point in wasting any more of his day on the search.

Chapter Three
Tuesday 14 September 1852 - Paris - Rue Marbeuf

Rougemont looked once more at the ornate clock that stood above the fireplace in the drawing-room on the first floor of the *hôtel* in the Rue Marbeuf which he had been renting for the last three months. Time was dragging, and he could not expect to see his guests from England for at least another hour. He paced the room. There was wine aplenty in the cellar, but he fought off the urge to broach another bottle before they arrived.

Louis Rougemont was half-way through man's allotted span of threescore years and ten. Until the age of twenty-five, he had kept the fresh-faced, clear-eyed look of a scholar near matriculation. Then the excesses of his life began to show themselves: too much wine, too many women attracted by the illusion of wealth he created, too much double-dealing with merchants owed money. When he was thirty, he looked like a man who had run through three decades without taking breath. And now, nearing thirty-five, his hair had thinned, his cheeks were gaunt and flushed red, and there was a nervous flicker to his eyes, as though he expected a bailiff to loom up at any moment and seize him by the shoulder.

It was four years since he had last spent time in Paris, before his credit with the taverns, and the women, finally ran out. That had been the time when he knew Franklin Blake, a younger man, but one in whom he recognised the taste and energy for indulgence which he had possessed at the same age. And Blake had money to buy the good things that Paris offered, and to share them with a companion like Rougemont who knew the hidden places where those *douceurs* could be found.

Since then, Blake had come into his family inheritance. Not Rougemont: he cursed his father's name, as he did every day. Henri Rougemont had prospered during Bonaparte's wars, supplying the army with boots and other footwear, buying them cheap from manufactures in France and elsewhere, and selling them dear, with payments to quartermasters that smoothed the transactions. After 1815, peace threatened to ruin him; but, turning his coat and his trade quickly, he made himself useful to the returning Bourbons and their *émigrés* followers by hiring himself out as a peripatetic land agent, and helping the counts and dukes who had lived in England for twenty years to seize back their old estates from the *arrivistes* who had moved in after the Revolution.

The work not only gave him a good living, it also introduced him to the woman he married. Lucinda Peverill was an English governess taken on by an *émigré* family in exile, brought back to France, and then released from their service after two years when their child reached maturity. Louis was born twelve months after the marriage; raised by his mother as

Lewis, it was thanks to her that he spoke English as well as French.

The Rougemonts prospered as long as the Bourbons reigned, and declined after their fall in 1830. Lucinda perished in the cholera outbreak in Paris in 1832; and, as Louis progressed towards manhood, he saw how his father struggled to maintain their household, stripped of the support of his wife and his aristocratic patrons. Acting once more as an intermediary in buying and selling goods, now between France and Britain, he faced stiff competition from the new breed of *bourgeois* entrepreneurs that were emerging under Louis-Philippe. Shortly after his sixtieth birthday, in 1846, Henri de Rougemont collapsed in the streets of Paris and was brought home, dead of exhaustion.

His legacy to Louis was better than his son allowed, but far worse than he had hoped. There were no debts, but no wealth either, other than the income he could earn from the commercial contacts which his father had established for him. Louis continued to act as an intermediary, but he lacked both Henri's skill, and his commitment. He needed money to maintain his way of life, but the idea of earning it as a supply agent filled him with contempt: he resented his father's assumption that he would simply step into the dead man's shoes and scamper to and fro in pursuit of clients. Far better, he reckoned, to ingratiate himself with British visitors to Paris and benefit from their willingness to spend money.

Blake had been one of his successes, and he had enjoyed his company, and his money, for weeks, if not months, until the Englishman's embroilment with that little actress had ended in tears, and Blake ran away from Paris like a scalded cat. Touchingly, Rougemont had received a letter written in haste by the Englishman just before he boarded a stage-coach for Brussels, in which Blake thanked Rougemont for the society that they had shared in the city, and voiced the hope that they might meet again "when passions had calmed". The Frenchman laughed inwardly at the naivety of the man.

There were other visitors from Albion whom Rougemont had been able to charm, even as they unknowingly let themselves be used by him to keep his finances above the water-line. His genteel work of money-extraction might have continued up to the present, except that, four years ago, Paris had another one of its twenty-year fits, threw the king out of the country, and fell back towards the state of anarchy that it had taken to extremes during the French Revolution of the 1790s. There was a good deal of bloody fighting, death and destruction. Rougemont didn't give a fig about what sort of government ruled France, but he was driven to despair by the cowardice of the British who simply stopped crossing the Channel when they heard about the turmoil in Paris. Without British visitors, Rougemont could no longer sustain a living in the French capital. He was forced to find employment; and, having disdained the work done by his father, he followed his mother's example by getting taken on as an English tutor by a wealthy family in the countryside near Reims.

It was not long before Rougemont decided that he hated this work, and himself for submitting to it; but, by keeping such thoughts to himself, he found that the family became fond of him and retained him, year after year. He settled into the routine, helped by ready access to the family's wine-cellar: if they knew that he spent most evenings drinking in his room, they said nothing about it.

The approach by Ledouin came out of the blue in the spring of that year. It was unusual enough that he received a letter: he had made little effort to keep his Paris contacts informed of his whereabouts. But it beggared belief that the correspondent knew so much about his earlier life, and should wish to discuss it face-to-face. After four years of provincial somnolence, Rougemont felt no immediate impulse to accede to the request; but Ledouin's written offer to entertain him at one of the better hostelries in Reims, as well as a wish to find out how the man had tracked him down, won out over inertia.

Rougemont rode in to Reims one Saturday in April, and listened to Ledouin over several courses, and a couple of bottles of *pinot noir*. Ledouin made no secret of the fact that he was an investigation agent, or that it was his interest in Franklin Blake that had led him to Rougemont: more than one of the actresses from the high days of 1847 remembered Louis with affection, Ledouin told him, and regretted that they hadn't seen him for so long. It hadn't been easy to discover where he had gone, but Ledouin had spoken to M. Sainclair, his old Paris landlord, who recalled a visit from his former tenant in the summer of 1848 to collect a few stored belongings. Rougemont told Sainclair about his position with a family near Reims, and in the end that was enough for Ledouin to run him to ground. Three glasses of *vin rouge* left Louis highly impressed, and he toasted Ledouin's achievement.

There remained the question of why Ledouin was interested in Blake. After testing Rougemont's feelings about the Englishman, and hearing him speak mockingly about Blake's farewell letter, Ledouin saw little risk that finer feelings would hold Rougemont back from the role which the investigation agent wanted him to play. So as to advance the design of his wealthy client in London, Ledouin said, he needed to ensure that Franklin Blake would return to Paris. How better than if Rougemont invited his former drinking companion back – to stay with him in circumstances of comfort which he, Ledouin, was authorised to pay for: a fine house in Paris, well-provisioned with food and drink and the appropriate serving staff, at the disposal of Rougemont for a period of six months? And there would of course be a retainer for Rougemont on top of his enjoyment of the accommodation.

It took Louis more than a few seconds, as well as half a glass of wine, to absorb the proposal. But, remarkable though it was, he could think of no ground to reject it: and he agreed. And, to the surprise of both men, his mind leapt momentarily into activity, and he disclosed to Ledouin a particular reason, a transaction that had taken place between Blake and himself in 1847, which he could summon up to make it all the more likely that the Englishman would accept the invitation. The investigation agent smiled his appreciation and stored the disclosure away, re-filled Rougemont's glass, and guided the meal to an amicable conclusion. The Frenchman stayed that night in one of the hostelry's rooms, and slept more soundly than in years. Ledouin slipped away into the darkness, undertaking to make the arrangements for Rougemont to start his new life in June.

And now it was three months since he had left the family in Reims, claiming that he had suddenly received an inheritance from a remote cousin; taken up residence in the Rue Marbeuf; and written as directed to Franklin Blake in England, feigning a burning desire for a reunion alongside a wish to deal again with that old transaction. It was two months since he received Blake's reply: a letter which began discouragingly, by explaining his situation as a married man with a young child, and asserting that he had turned his back on the excesses of his youth - only to end with a confirmation that he and his beloved wife would take up the invitation, in the confident expectation that they would rejoice in seeing his old companion, his fine-sounding residence, and Paris. And it was at least an hour since he had found the wait for his guests unbearable.

Rougemont paced across the salon again and looked through the windows down to the street below. Surely they must arrive soon: but no, the clock showed him that he must be patient still.

Somewhere out there he knew that Ledouin was waiting as well. For so long as Rougemont had continued in his role as tutor to the family near Reims, the investigation agent had communicated with him by letters, sent from

London. But he had been in Paris to see Rougemont installed in his rented splendour, and to ensure that he did not delay in writing to Blake. He had travelled back the day after receiving a missive from the Frenchman, saying that Blake had accepted his invitation; and then he spent several hours with Rougemont, discussing the preparations that must be made by September. He left the Frenchman with a closely written record of all these, so that nothing would be overlooked. Letters continued to flow from the office in Bethnal Green Cut to the house in Rue Marbeuf until, two days before the scheduled arrival of Mr and Mrs Blake, Ledouin appeared once more in the French capital. Admitted to the house, he monopolised Rougemont for half a day, sitting opposite him on the deep-cushioned chairs in the salon, and coaching him in the role that he would have to play.

As he left, emphasising that his own stay in Paris would last as long as the Blakes' and that he would be close at hand throughout, he handed over the latest instalment of the retainer. Rougemont sat for some time, counting the money over. It was balm to his soul, and soothed the irritation that he felt at being so closely instructed by this inescapable Englishman. He didn't regret agreeing to act for him: how else would his circumstances have improved so much? But he had not foreseen that he would be shadowed so insistently by Ledouin. He had put on a good act, for Franklin Blake and others, only four or five years previously, and he really needed no lessons in the art. But money talked, and the retainer told him clearly that Ledouin's words were paramount.

The clock chimed six times, and suddenly Rougemont heard a clatter of hooves in the street below. A carriage stopped; the driver was speaking to his passengers; doors were opening and closing. After looking through the window again, he hurried downstairs.

The two male servants hired by Ledouin were already in attendance: Guillaume, the steward, was helping Jean, the young footman, to transfer the travellers' luggage from carriage to house. The new arrivals came down the carriage steps and looked round.

Rougemont strode to greet them. "Franklin," he called warmly. "I am delighted to see you again", and he shook Blake's hand. The vigour with which Blake responded, the brightness of his eyes, and the newness of the clothes that he wore, all showed a man in his prime.

"Lewis, my dear friend, I am equally pleased to see you in such fine fettle." If Blake noticed the deterioration in Rougemont's looks, he disguised the fact well. Hands were shaken all over again. "Forgive me for neglecting you for so many years – but, as you see, I have been much engaged in matters of family. Lewis, this is my beloved wife, Rachel."

Rougemont turned to the young woman at Blake's side. Shorter than both men by at least a head, her black hair framed a face that was exquisitely pretty, with dark eyes that now rested on the Frenchman with a gaze that was both friendly and searching. She wore a red travelling cape that enclosed her, Rougemont thought, like a precious stone in a jewel box. He kissed her hand

and said: "I am indebted to you for allowing your husband to make this visit, Madame Blake. I hope that you will not be disappointed by your stay in Paris."

"Franklin has told me so much that I feel almost as though I have been here before," she said, with laughter in her voice. "But I wanted to see the city for myself, even if it meant being parted from our little daughter for a week."

"She is in good hands in London, my dear," Blake said, kissing his wife's hand as well. "As I said, Lewis, our family has filled the last few years. It seems far longer since I was here."

"And this is Penelope, my maid," Rachel said, indicating the third member of the party. The maid bobbed briefly in acknowledgement; Rougemont saw almost a mirror image of Blake's wife, though dressed in a less vivid coat. "Neither Penelope nor I know much French, Monsieur Rougemont. I am pleased indeed to hear you speak English so well."

"I was fortunate to be born to an English mother, who taught me well."

"And your father?" Rachel asked.

"He was French. He taught me very little – except perhaps the pleasures of the table." He smiled. Guillaume and Jean had removed all the bags from the carriage. "But, please, let us go in. You must be tired from travelling. Your rooms await you. We shall dine in two hours, unless that is too soon."

"That will be perfect, Lewis. Perfect." Blake shook hands for a third time, and they entered the house. Guillaume showed the guests to their rooms.

Rougemont took refuge in the drawing-room again, and slumped into one of the yielding arm-chairs. Blake was as he remembered him, still with a boyish charm that was pleasant and preposterous in equal measure. He could play him now with the same ease as when they last met. But Mrs Franklin Blake was a different matter. Behind her friendly gaze he had sensed a seriousness and a sobriety that suggested a much less pliable character than her husband. It was a form of the reserve and self-possession that he always associated with Englishwomen, above all with his mother. The presence in Paris of Blake's wife threatened complications that he and Ledouin had not foreseen.

The door from the stairway opened suddenly and broke his train of thought. It was Blake, who strode across and sat down next to him. "Lewis, my dear man, it is marvellous to find you prospering. Look at the splendours of this house." He glanced around at the fine furnishings in the room, at the paintings hanging on the walls, and at the cabinets full of porcelain.

"I am still getting used to them, Franklin," Rougemont replied. "It is only a few months since I came into my inheritance. I took this place on only as a provisional arrangement, until I decide how to arrange my affairs for the future."

"Yes, how quickly our lives can change. When last we met, I was a nomad, roaming from one country to the next without a fixed purpose. And now, only four or five years later, I am the head of a household, with a wife and child, and a future shaped by service to my family and to my country." He paused, and Rougemont wondered whether he caught a note of regret in the Englishman's voice. "Lewis, I wanted to speak to you alone, while my dear wife is settling into her accommodation and preparing for dinner tonight." He leaned towards the Frenchman. "As you asked in your letter, I have brought with me the object which you sold me when I was last in Paris. You wish to buy it back?"

Rougemont paused for a moment, remembering Ledouin's advice not to press Blake too hard. "You know that it belonged to my father, who acquired it honestly, but in unusual circumstances? I would not have sold it to you, except that my resources were then at a very low ebb. But now that I am better placed, I would be keen to reverse the transaction, and have it in my hands again, as a keepsake, for my father's memory." Ledouin had approved the script. "But we need not discuss the matter immediately, Franklin. This is your first evening in Paris, and you shouldn't cloud it with business matters."

Blake, leaning back in his chair, seemed momentarily distracted. "No, no, you're right." He looked at Rougemont again. "But tell me how it came into your father's possession."

Rougemont nodded, indulgently. "In the last fifteen years of his life, my father spent more time travelling

57

up and down the highways of France than he did in our house in Paris. He was forever making agreements with manufacturers in Lyons, in Nantes or in Marseilles, and signing up counter-parties in your own country. And, as well as acting like a dog that is always chasing its tail, he had a magpie's fascination for little curios – mostly of no value at all, but sometimes..." Rougemont left the words hanging.

"I see. And this object, how did he acquire it?"

"He was in Brittany, not for the first time. He had struck an agreement with a Breton notable to supply crushed sea-shells, for some manufacturing process, I never knew what. On his second or third visit there, he discovered that the notable had died, and his widow was struggling to make ends meet. My father saw the object on display in her house, offered her a good price for it, and brought it home."

"But how did such an exotic treasure come to appear in a house in Brittany?"

"As to that..." Rougemont began. But the door opened again and a head appeared: it was the maid.

"Begging your pardon, Mr Blake, Mr Rougemont..."

"Penelope?" Blake queried. "What is it? Come in, do. You don't mind, do you, Lewis?"

The young woman took two or three steps into the room. "My lady apologises for troubling you, but she asks if you would be good enough to give her your advice."

"Willingly," Blake replied. "But about what?"

Penelope glanced down, smiling. "It's a matter of costume, sir."

Blake jumped up, shook Rougemont's hand again vigorously, and said: "Not to be delayed, I fear. We'll pick up our conversation again soon, my dear Lewis." He left the room, with the maid going on ahead.

Rougemont began to pace the room again. Yes, Mrs Blake was definitely proving a complication. If he'd been able to continue their exchange for just five or ten more minutes...

How would he have answered Blake's question? Not with the truth, which his father had confided in him before his death. Not with the secret that the Breton widow had told Henri Rougemont, that this was a treasure looted from the Charles X museum when rioters broke into the Louvre in July 1830, part of the uprising that forced the Bourbons from power. And that among the looters who stuffed their pockets with objects from the Egyptian galleries and ran off into the city was a close friend of her late husband, who later sold him the ill-gotten curio.

It was a pendant, a frame of finely worked silver which formed a figure of eight around two blood-red carnelian stones – one, the head, half the size of the other, the body – and extended at either side into wings that were inset with short strips of shaped glass. It was a bee made of precious metal and jewels, brought back from the sands of Egypt by the expedition which the first Napoléon had led to that country at the turn of the century. Never mind that the stones that formed the head and the body glowed with a dark crimson light: it was unmistakably a bee. In the five decades since then, it had been in Paris, then in Brittany, in Paris again, in England, and now at last it had once more returned to Paris.

It was not the wish to honour his father's memory that drove Rougemont's desire to buy the pendant back from Blake. For all that he spurned his father's wheeling and dealing, Rougemont thought that he knew a money-making opportunity when he saw one. And the inauguration of a Second Empire, which everyone in France expected to happen soon, was just such an opportunity. Egypt was part of the Bonapartist legend; the bee was Napoléon's dynastic symbol. He was sure that he would find an eager buyer for the pendant among the wider entourage of Bonaparte's nephew who was about to take back the imperial crown.

He regretted telling Ledouin about the pendant, though the investigation agent was happy enough that Rougemont should use his wish to buy it back as another reason for Blake to come to Paris. But he knew that Ledouin was following his own plan for what was to happen to Blake in the city: he needed to induce Blake to part with the pendant before the Englishman was consumed by that plan.

He saw no more of his visitors before the time came for the evening meal, served in the dining-room which was adjacent to the salon. With little enough guidance from Rougemont, Guillaume had ensured that all was ready: the food prepared in the kitchen by the cook and her assistant; the wine decanted and set out on a buffet; the table laid with glass and metalware for three people, and decorated with a centrepiece of flowers bought from the market earlier that day.

Franklin and Rachel Blake appeared in the drawing-room: he wore a dark-green half-length coat, over a gold-coloured waistcoat, with a neckerchief of green silk flecked with yellow; while she wore a dress that was trimmed with lace around the neck, cinched at the waist and then billowed out to brush against the floor – and which seemed to fill the room with the warmth of its scarlet glow. The two were smiling, at themselves as much as at Rougemont, their host felt; but he felt as well that, if he were married to a woman like Mrs Blake, he would be smiling too.

And it was Rachel who spoke first, even as Rougemont was gathering his thoughts. "Good evening, or *bonsoir*, M. Rougemont. You see, I am trying to learn some French." Now her smile was directed just at him.

"It is very good of you, Madame Blake --"

"Please, call me Rachel. I know that you and Franklin are old friends."

Rougemont inclined his head briefly. "I am honoured, Rachel. Please, allow me to show you both the way."

They walked through to sit at table. Rougemont gave little heed to the meal that was served by Guillaume but, on Ledouin's advice, it was both suited to an English palate – a mildly flavoured *potage de légumes*, a small plate of chicken-breast baked with mushroom and herbs, a flourish of beef with root vegetables, and a dessert of berries with *crème anglaise* – and cooked to perfection.

The two men drank freely from the wine that Guillaume served: Rachel's first glass was still half-full when the dessert was served.

Whether it was the wine, or the intimate conviviality of the dinner, Rougemont quickly found that his apprehensions vanished and that he slipped with ease into his role of host and old friend. He encouraged his guests to talk about their life in London. Blake gave an account of the elections which had happened only two months before, and which had allowed Lord Derby to form a Government that, according to Blake, wanted to turn the clock back on the economic advances that the country had made in recent years. After several minutes of this, Rougemont pretended to display impatience, and asked Rachel, with Blake's blessing, to say more about their family life. The young woman explained how, little more than a year earlier, she had given birth to their first child, a little girl they had called Julia, after her own mother; and how they had followed their child's progress over the intervening months, through crawling to taking her first steps.

"And she is every bit as beautiful as her mother," Blake assured Rougemont, making Rachel blush. "It was a wrench to leave her behind us in London, but we did so want to take up your invitation, and I doubt that Julia would have had much appreciation of the journey."

"And I mean to take a souvenir of Paris back with me, to give to Julia when we return home. What might you suggest, Lewis?"

"Ah, that is a difficult question for a man who knows little or nothing about young children. If she were ten years older or more, you could take something pretty, like a ring, or a bracelet, or..." He paused, sensing that Blake was looking at him with a sudden intensity. "...or a fine silk scarf. But for such a young child?"

Rachel had missed the glance from her husband at their host, and spoke with laughter in her voice. "Fine silk, yes, Julia loves to play with colourful fabrics. You must tell me where I can buy one."

"I can tell you of several shops, only a short ride from here. And how is life in London? Have you always lived there?"

"Oh no. For most of my life, before Franklin and I were married three years ago, I lived two hundred miles north of London, in Yorkshire."

"Yorkshire?" Rougemont repeated the name, quizzically. "Is that also a city?"

Both his guests laughed. "Far from it," said Blake.

"There is an ancient city of York, but Yorkshire itself is a county, miles and miles of fine countryside with many smaller towns and villages scattered across it. My family home is near a place called Frizinghall."

"Frizing Hall? Is it called that because the weather is freezing there?"

More laughter. "Forgive us," Rachel said. "It is true that the winters can be hard in Yorkshire. But my mother told me that frizing was an old-fashioned word for cloth made of wool, and that Frizinghall used to be well-known for making that cloth."

"I see." Rougemont was smiling as well, catching the amusement of the others. "And perhaps all that woollen cloth was needed because of the freezing winters?"

"Very good!" Blake hooted. "Don't you agree, Rachel? Two good reasons for Frizinghall to be given the name it has." He raised his glass. "Here's to good Yorkshire wool, and honest Yorkshire frost!" Both men drank deeply: Rachel only sipped from her glass, but her eyes were sparkling with the good humour of their conversation.

"Franklin has told me that, with your help, he has drawn up a plan of the sights that we are to see here in Paris, starting tomorrow. I am greatly looking forward to it."

"There is much to see," Rougemont responded, "and it would be unwise to attempt too much in a single day.

So tomorrow I have arranged that a carriage will take you to visit the Louvre, and the wonderful museums that it contains, including the Musée des Antiques, the Musée Grec et Romain, the Galerie Assyrienne and the Galerie Egyptienne."

"Four museums under one roof!"

"There are even more than that, my dear," Blake said, "but if we complete our inspection of those four, we shall have done very well indeed! But Lewis, my old friend, will you not accompany us?"

"Only as far as the entrance, dear friends, to be sure that you gain admittance. But then I must return here, to deal with matters of administration."

"My head may be spinning after so much antiquity," Rachel laughed. "Shall we be there all day?"

"Have no fear," Blake said. "Lewis has recommended a fine new restaurant not far from the Palais du Louvre, where we shall take our luncheon. And in the afternoon we shall drive to the Bois de Boulogne."

At Rachel's quizzical look, Rougemont explained: "Our Prince-President has directed that a vast area to the west of the city should be turned into a magnificent new park, where citizens can take their leisure, on foot, on horseback or in carriages. The work is well advanced."

"It is intended to be the Hyde Park of Paris, my dear," Blake added. "And, after what may prove a somewhat dusty study of old marble statues, what could be better than an afternoon ride along the tree-lined avenues of the Bois?"

"It sounds marvellous," the young woman replied. The dessert had been served and eaten, and Rachel finally drank what little wine remained in her glass. "And now, Lewis, if you will excuse me, I shall retire to my room. This has been a wonderful meal, for which I thank you. But I confess that the day has wearied me, and I need to be rested and ready for tomorrow!" She got up from the table.

"As you wish, Rachel," said her host. "Franklin, you may also be tired --"

But Rachel interrupted. "No, you two old friends should take the opportunity to catch up with each other. I am perfectly able to find my way through your house, Lewis. And I shall not want for company. Penelope, my maid, is a quite unstoppable chatterbox!"

"A chatterbox?" Rougemont queried.

His visitors laughed. "She means that, in the art of conversation, Penelope has particular talent," Blake explained. The three of them walked back across the drawing-room. He smiled at his wife. "Off you go then, my dear, but don't allow Penelope's prattling to tire you even more."

"Good night, Lewis, and thank you again." With a last smile, she turned away from the men; moving swiftly and elegantly in her red dress, she moved to the door and was gone.

Rougemont saw how Blake's gaze lingered on the closed door for seconds after his wife had left. Then he spoke: "A cigar, Franklin?"

"Sorry?" queried the other man, coming back to himself. "Well, yes, I think that would answer well to this superb evening, thank you."

Rougemont offered him a cigar from a gilded box, helped him light it, and placed a glass of cognac by his elbow, as Blake settled into an armchair. With his own cigar and brandy, he sat opposite him. There was silence initially, as the two men savoured the smoke.

"And is it really only five years since I last saw you, Lewis? It seems a lifetime ago."

"Only five years – but your life has changed completely since then."

It took the Englishman some time to reply. "Completely, yes, to the last degree. What a wonder! And yours too, Lewis. Five years ago, yours was a hand-to-mouth existence, was it not. And now, look at your circumstances." Rougemont, who knew the truth of his circumstances, felt a flicker of discomfort. But Blake noticed nothing, for he suddenly jumped up from his chair and went to the window. "And look at the city out there." Night had fallen, and the view from the window showed a filigree of lights sparkling in the darkness. Rougemont stood by his side. "How mysterious it looks under night's shadow. Mysterious, and intriguing." He rested his forehead against the glass.

The Frenchman looked at him. "But Franklin, do you want to go out into the night-time streets?"

Blake drew deeply on his cigar, then exhaled. "A lifetime ago, I would have said yes." He swallowed his cognac in one go. "But not now, my old friend." He returned Rougemont's gaze. "How good it is to be here again. Tomorrow, once day has returned, that will be the right time for exploring this city. And for completing our transaction. Now, though, I must leave you, with gratitude and friendship, and rejoin my dear wife. You understand, don't you Lewis?"

"Of course, Franklin." They shook hands warmly and once again Rougemont was left alone in the drawing-room. "Tomorrow," he said to himself. "Tomorrow may bring all manner of things to pass."

Chapter Four
Tuesday 14 September 1852 - Bourges

It was a sleepy town one hundred and fifty miles south of Paris, that had seen little excitement since the fifteenth century, when it flourished as the court of the Duc de Berry. Once that court faded, Bourges settled back into a quiet provincial obscurity. But today was different.

The Prince-President, Louis-Napoléon, was beginning an official tour of the southern regions of France, to test public opinion about the regime which he had ushered in with the *coup d'état* of December 1851. Bourges was the starting-point. The dusty streets of the town, normally empty except for the occasional horse-drawn cart, were now brimming with crowds of people who had walked there from the surrounding countryside. Many had come the day before and, too numerous for the town's hotels and taverns, had spent the night under makeshift covers in the squares and courtyards.

The nephew of the great Emperor arrived by train, and rode from the station on horseback, accompanied by a large retinue of counsellors and dignitaries, and a contingent of foot-soldiers to underline the importance of the visitor – and to be ready to put down any hostile agitation. It was still less than a year since the *coup.* Much of the most violent resistance to the seizure of power had broken out in the south of France – not in Bourges, but in the cities of Lyon and Marseilles which lay further along his itinerary. Louis-Napoléon wanted to show himself to France outside Paris and, while he never doubted the attachment of the French to the legacy of Bonapartist glory, he could not take it for granted that they welcomed the embodiment of that legacy in his own person.

But riding at the Prince-President's side was a man who had left nothing to chance: Victor Vicomte de Persigny, Louis-Napoléon's oldest ally, and Minister of the Interior since Morny stood down in early 1852. Persigny had argued most strongly for the tour of the south, and he had used all the resources of his office – money, patronage, threats – to ensure an enthusiastic reception in Bourges and in the towns that were to follow. Flags with Napoleonic emblems fluttered from the main buildings, and a massive Imperial eagle, carved out of wood, had been fixed above the main gate to the town. Persigny was pleased with the work of his agents.

The crowds of country-folk were impressed by the day's pomp, and by the spectacle of their Prince-President riding through their midst; but it was the regime's loyalists who started up the shouts of "*Vive Napoléon*" and even "*Vive l'Empereur!*" which engulfed the procession as they made their way to the old cathedral of Saint-Étienne, for a service of thanksgiving led by the Archbishop. Louis-Napoléon's face was often a mask of inscrutability. Today, however, Persigny, and everyone else, could see that face animated by an expression of delight in his reception by the ordinary people thronging the streets.

The cathedral service was followed by a supper for the distinguished visitor at the Archbishop's Palace; even as Rougemont, Blake and his wife enjoyed their intimate dinner in the Rue Marbeuf, Louis-Napoléon sat at a grand table laid for two dozen diners. Finally, in the late evening, the visit culminated in a celebratory ball hosted by the Prefect at the Hôtel de Ville. Persigny's efforts ensured that, wherever he went, the Prince-President was cheered to the echo by the thousands who still packed the town – and who were rewarded not only by the sight of the great man, but also by a firework display that marked the end of the ball.

Louis-Napoléon himself, with the Prefect, the Archbishop and a score of local notables, watched the display seated on a specially built platform in the garden of the Hôtel de Ville. Persigny sat behind him, and allowed himself to relax for the first time in a long day. His gaze turned away from the streaks of light in the sky overhead, and towards the crowds: as he had known all along, if they were given spectacle and colour, they would be captured and kept. The Republic was dull and insipid, and had no place in the hearts of the French: that belonged to the Empire, and the day when it would be re-born was drawing near.

It was as he turned these thoughts over, and as the last fireworks burst across the sky, that one of the Prefect's aides hurried on to the platform, recognised Persigny, and passed him a folded sheet of paper. The recipient read the brief message. At once, he leaned forward to pass on the news to the Prince-President, who turned his head to hear clearly.

"Your Excellency," Persigny said, "Lord Wellington died today, in London."

The light show ended. The streets around still rang with the shouts of the crowd, but Louis-Napoléon and his loyal Minister seemed isolated in a moment of calm and silence. The Prince-President twisted his moustache gently, then said: "It is a sign. Our old enemy is gone – may God rest his soul. The way ahead is clear." He stood up and, followed dutifully by the others on the platform, strode purposefully back into the Hôtel de Ville.

Wednesday 15 September 1852 – Paris - Rue Marbeuf

Franklin Blake and his wife arrived back in the Rue Marbeuf at the end of the afternoon with their heads full of the sights of the city. They had lingered in the museums of the Louvre, enjoyed a leisurely meal in the little restaurant nearby, and then driven at length through the Bois de Boulogne, stopping from time to time so that Rachel could run across the lawns and allow Franklin to catch up with her.

Rougemont kept to his word, going with them to guide them into the Louvre, but leaving them there "because two are company, and three are none", as he told them. He went straight back to his house; and, within five minutes of stepping inside, found that Ledouin had noted his return and gained admittance to the drawing-room where he sat. Rougemont reported all that had taken place over the previous twenty-four hours; Ledouin set out in great detail what was to ensue, and left again well before noon.

And so it was that Rougemont did not share the surprise that troubled Blake when, after seeing his wife to their room and then looking in on his host as a courtesy, he found that a letter had been left for him during his absence.

"But who on earth knows that I am a guest in your house?" Blake asked, as he pulled open the letter. He fell suddenly silent as he glanced over the writing, then sat down heavily in one of the arm-chairs. He groaned softly. "How can this be?"

"Franklin?" Rougemont asked, voicing concern and puzzlement. "What is it?" There was no response: the Englishman seemed stunned. "Franklin?"

Blake said nothing, but thrust the letter towards the other man. Rougemont read the message, that had been written in French.

"Monsieur Blake. I had thought never to meet you again. I was wrong. I saw you arrive in Paris yesterday. But you failed to see me. You had eyes only for the young woman who was with you. She can only be your wife. I followed you. I wanted to be certain that it was you and, if it was, to demand that you see me again.

"You may wish to forget how you treated me before. I cannot. I gave you so much, and got so little back. For years I have tried to forget. Seeing you has made that impossible. If you come to me, if you give me back what you took from me, I will at last forgive you. Otherwise I shall come to you, and tell the world how you treated me. I shall wait for you, this evening, in the Auberge des Dunes, Rue de Calais. Do not fail me again – and do not doubt my seriousness. Suzanne Pâquerette"

Blake was still slumped in his chair, struck dumb. "What will you do?" Rougemont asked. There was no answer. "Franklin, you cannot ignore this. You cannot risk this woman coming here."

The Englishman jumped to his feet. "By God, I cannot! I must go and see her, and go tonight!" He seemed poised to hurry out of the house.

"And your wife, Franklin?"

"Rachel?" He stood stock still. "Rachel?"

"Does she know about --" Rougemont paused, "-- about the life you led in Paris?"

"Oh yes," he assured him. "That is, she knows that I ran up debts by entertaining imprudent companions." Blake was oblivious to the slight that his words gave to his host.

"Female companions? And this one in particular?"

Blake fixed him with his gaze: momentary anger gave way to flickering despair. "Lewis, will you stand by me? I shall go and explain all to my dear wife. But then, will you come with me to this accursed meeting? In that damnable inn, of all places!"

"I will stand by you, of course." There was a fervent shaking of hands. "But, Franklin, though I will accompany you there, I cannot share in your conversation with this woman. That must be for you alone."

Blake's head fell. "You are right. Ready yourself, Lewis. We shall leave in an hour." The Englishman took a deep breath, and walked out of the room.

Rougemont stood at the window and looked out at the gathering shadows. It was shaping up as Ledouin had said that it would, hastening towards the outcome that the investigation agent had planned. For a moment, Rougemont had an image of his payment as thirty pieces of silver. Blake's words about imprudent companions came back to him, and the image dissolved. He would have his payment, but he also meant to prise the pendant from him before the opportunity was lost.

When an hour later the two men left the house in Rue Marbeuf, riding across Paris in a carriage, no more words passed between them. Blake was lost in his own thoughts, his gloom deepened by the explanation that he had been forced to give his young wife. Rougemont's efforts to draw him into conversation failed utterly; in silence, in darkness, they drove towards the encounter in the Rue de Calais.

Paris - Rue de Calais

It was a week since Lucien de Boizillac had chased Cotte, and lost him. Though Delourcq had been obliged to stay at home and let his leg recover, Boizillac had not been idle. On both the Thursday and Friday after Cotte's disappearance, he returned to the streets on either side of the Canal Saint-Martin to check if he could see with his own eyes, or hear from any of the locals, any evidence that Cotte had dragged himself from the water and found a hiding-place down some back alley.

After two days, and with no result, Boizillac made his way to the Quai Morland, on the right bank of the Seine as it flowed through the centre of the city. The turgid surface of the river was some way below the embanked quay, and looking down Boizillac could see the bastard boat, half-barge, half-shack, that was moored below. It belonged to Gustave Taillefer, one of the city's oldest river-scavengers. Taillefer was no man's friend; but he had saved Boizillac's life the year before, and nursed him back to health when the young man had been beaten senseless and thrown into the water.

Boizillac climbed down the flight of stone sills that projected from the embanked wall and stepped on to the deck of the boat. "Taillefer?" he called.

A door in the floating shack opened, and an old man came out. "Captain Boizillac," he grumbled. "On your own?"

"Today, yes. Delourcq was injured earlier this week."

"I heard about that. He has old bones already. They break more easily." Taillefer drew on the pipe that he was smoking. "But he'll live?"

"He'll live," Boizillac confirmed. "I wanted to ask you something." The old man was silent. "You know how Delourcq came by his injury?"

"Got in someone's way, I heard."

"Jacques Cotte. You know the name?"

"I do now. Not a friend of the Government?"

"He wasn't before this week, and he's likely to be even less friendly now, if he's still alive." Boizillac moved a pace closer to the old man, and lowered his voice. "He was shot and went headlong into the canal. But there's been no body recovered. And no-one in the streets around the Place de Marais admits to seeing him since then. Have you heard anything, Taillefer?"

"I've heard what happens to the unfortunates who get taken away for speaking up against this regime. That's if they're not shot first."

"Just between you and me, Taillefer, I don't like hunting these men down either. But if I don't do it, someone else will. And in Cotte's case, he forfeited my goodwill when he almost broke Delourcq's leg. I'm sorry if he's drowned in the canal. But I'm not sure he has. So, have you heard anything?"

The other man drew on his pipe, and breathed the smoke out. "It was Wednesday, wasn't it?" Boizillac nodded. "I heard one of the bargees checked his boat the next morning, and found blood-stains under a cargo-cover."

"Did he report it?"

"Why would he do that? He just threw a bucket of water over it and sailed back up the canal."

"It must have been Cotte. But he wasn't on the barge?" Taillefer shook his head. "Then he's still in Paris somewhere."

"I'd wish you luck in finding him, for Delourcq's sake. But it'll be like looking for a rat in a sewer."

"Thanks for the information." He shook the old man's hand. "I'll keep looking."

"Watch out for Graize." Boizillac looked questioningly at him. "Alfred Graize, police inspector. The Saint-Martin quarter, where your man went missing, is his patch, or has been for the last year. Haven't you met him?"

"No, though I've heard his name."

"He's a sight for sore eyes. Bald as a coot, with a black beard down to his chest. Stands a head taller than most men. Hard as nails with anyone he thinks has committed a crime. And hard as nails with everyone else as well. Be careful if your paths cross. He'll try and walk all over you."

The conversation ended. Boizillac took his leave and climbed back up to the quay. Taillefer stayed on the deck of his barge for a minute or two, smoking his pipe, then retreated into the cabin.

That had been Friday: it was Wednesday now. In the intervening days, Boizillac had been caught up in other cases. But what Taillefer told him left little doubt in his mind that Cotte survived being shot and was again in hiding. He decided to make one more visit to the Place des Marais and its environs. Perhaps the onset of evening and the deepening shadows would make it more likely that someone would pass information to him. Not for the first time, he regretted Delourcq's absence.

He had spent an hour or more going in and out of inns and bars on the west side of the canal. He tried the drinkers at the Wauxhall ball-room, only a few score paces from the hovel where they had surprised Cotte, but without success. In the distance, he heard a church bell strike nine. It was as he turned back towards the canal, following the Rue Grange, that he noticed a small side-street opposite, the Rue de Calais, hinged to the larger road by a tavern, the *Auberge des Dunes*. He could hear raised voices coming from it and, as he looked more closely through the street window, he saw a tall figure inside, with a shiny pate and a great beard spilling down his front. The man was at the bar, talking loudly with the inn-keeper. "Alfred Graize," Boizillac said to himself, remembering Taillefer's description. "Let's see if he can tell me anything."

His entrance into the inn went unnoticed at first. All eyes were on Graize. Glancing round, Boizillac saw that there were several drinkers at most of the tables, but at a couple of them, at either side of the room, were two solitary drinkers: one, a younger man, stared fixedly towards the bar, with a look almost of panic; the other had better control of his eyes, but seemed intent on listening to the very public conversation that was underway.

"You fetched me here because two of your clients, a man and a woman, have locked themselves in your private dining-room and haven't come out for an hour?" Graize almost spat the words at the inn-keeper. "Don't you think I have better things to do, Ricord?" Jean-Marie Ricord was the first to spot the new arrival. He alerted Graize with a flick of his eyebrows. The policeman turned. "Who are you?" It was not a welcome.

"Lucien de Boizillac, of the Sûreté."

"Why are you poking around here?"

"Are you Alfred Graize? I wanted to have a word about an investigation."

"Here? Now? Can't it wait?"

80

Boizillac was about to answer when there was a sudden outburst of noise from behind a door to the right of the bar. There was a loud thud, of furniture being knocked over, amid a crash of breaking glass; then two or three further thuds were heard. Boizillac started towards the door, but was stopped by Graize. "This is nothing to do with you," the older man said. He tried the door, only to find that, after moving back no more than a hand's width, it was blocked. "Ricord, come and help me!" The inn-keeper sloped across; they both put their shoulders to the wood and pushed vigorously. With effort, they opened the door fully.

The obstacle had been the table: it now lay on its side, surrounded by fragments of bottles and drinking glasses. To the left, a candle burnt on a shelf, alongside a clock which showed that it was now five past nine. Ahead, at the back of the room, was another closed door. To the right was a shuttered window. But the centrepiece was formed by two bodies: an expensively dressed young man, who lay prostrate, and unmoving; and beneath him, on her back, a woman, her head thrown back unnaturally, her hair disordered, her eyes open and unseeing. Both were partly tangled up in a chair that had been knocked over.

Graize knelt down and checked both of them rapidly. "The woman is dead," he said, in a matter-of-fact way. "The man is unconscious, and full of alcohol. Ricord, who are these people?"

"The woman is called Suzanne Pâquerette. The man is English. His name is Blake."

81

"Who has come into this room since the two of them arrived here?"

"Only me," Ricord offered. "I brought them their wine half an hour ago. They didn't call for me after that."

Graize walked round the dining-room. "And this other door? What's behind it?"

"A store-room."

The police-man tried the door. "Locked. Who has the key to it?"

Ricord pointed to the key-ring attached to his belt. "Me. There's only one key, and this is it."

Graize came back and stood above the forms on the floor. "Help me move the man out of the way." They got Blake into a sitting position and dragged him so that he was propped against a wall. Graize looked more closely at the woman, focussing on her neck, exposed by the angle of her head and her torn bodice. Her skin was scratched and red. "Strangled." He had seen all he wanted of the crime scene.

Turning round, he looked back into the main area of the tavern. Boizillac stood at the door, and behind him were the others in the bar, who now stared at the devastation in the dining-room. The young drinker with the panic gaze was foremost. "Do any of you know these two?" Graize asked, brusquely. There was no response. "In that case, get back to your drinks and let me do my job!" They needed no second asking.

Boizillac had forgotten his own case. "How can I help you?"

Graize seemed discountenanced by the offer. "You help me? I'll be honest - you can best help me by leaving me to deal with this in my way. I'll take this drunken Englishman into custody, and see that he pays for his crime."

"You have no doubt that he is responsible?"

Graize stared at him. "A woman lies dead on the floor, strangled. A drunken man lies on top of her. No-one else has been in the room for an hour. Life is too short to have doubts where the facts are crystal clear. Boizillac, I wish you good night."

Against his own instincts, Boizillac did as he was told. Back in the bar-room, he noticed that the older of the two solitary drinkers had disappeared. The younger one stood by the street-door, as though undecided what to do, but the sight of Boizillac determined him. He left.

Impulsively, Boizillac decided to follow him. Graize had made it abundantly clear that his presence at the crime scene was unnecessary; and there was something furtive about the younger drinker's behaviour that piqued Boizillac's interest.

As he stepped out into the Rue de Calais, he looked either side of him and caught sight of two men some twenty paces away who seemed to be in conversation. But almost immediately they parted company. One hurried off on foot in the direction of the canal; the other waved to a carriage. It was the younger drinker. Even as he climbed up into the carriage, Boizillac ran over and jumped in beside him as the vehicle jolted into motion.

"My God! Who are you?"

"Lucien de Boizillac, captain of police. And who are you?"

"Me? Why do you want to know? And what right have you to jump into this carriage?"

"I was just in the *Auberge des Dunes*. So were you. I observed how you took fright when you saw the struggle that had taken place in the private room and ran away. That's not the behaviour of an innocent bystander. So, who are you?"

"Louis Rougemont."

"Thank you, Monsieur Rougemont. And do you know either the Englishman – Blake, I think is his name – or the woman?"

There was silence for a few moments. As they rumbled through the darkened streets, Boizillac waited for an answer. Rougemont slumped forward, his head in his hands, then spoke rapidly.

"The woman is no friend of mine. But Blake has been staying with me since yesterday."

"So why didn't you tell Graize? Why didn't you stay to help him?" There was no answer, beyond a quiet groan. "But you were with him when he went to the inn tonight?"

Rougemont looked up. "Blake – before he was married, he had a liaison with that woman. And this evening, he came to the *auberge* because she summoned him there."

"Why?"

"She threatened to expose their former liaison."

"And so he came here and attacked her?"

"Blake would never do that!" Rougemont put his hand to his brow again. "Never! I cannot understand what happened."

They were on the Boulevard Saint-Martin now. "Where are we going?" Boizillac asked.

"To my house in the Rue Marbeuf."

"And Blake and his wife are staying there with you?"

"My God!" Rougemont exclaimed. "His wife. What am I going to tell her?"

"Does she know where her husband went tonight, and who was waiting to see him?"

"He said that he had told her. But how am I to explain what has happened?"

Boizillac left the question in the air for a few moments. Then: "How do you explain it?"

Rougemont gave him a troubled look. "Me?"

"Yes. You know the Englishman, it seems. You just said that he would never attack the woman. And yet every appearance suggests that he just did so. Who else can offer an explanation?" The other man looked away, out of the carriage. "There was another drinker in the *auberge* who also left just before you. Do you know him?"

But Rougemont had become more guarded. "I know Blake, and I know the inn-keeper, from the time, some years ago, when Blake and I used to drink there." He huddled down against the seat of the carriage, offering nothing more.

Boizillac paused. "Monsieur Rougemont, your conduct this evening has hardly been that of a friend. An English visitor – and his wife – are guests in your house. You escort him to a dubious assignation and, when this meeting takes a sinister turn, and Mr Blake falls under suspicion of committing a murder, you run away." Though Rougemont said nothing, he looked at Boizillac with a mixture of disdain and fear. "I shall report back to Inspector Graize on what I have learnt, and he will no doubt want to talk to you as well."

"What will happen to Blake?"

"Graize will place him in a police cell, and a trial will follow." The other man put his head in his hands again. Boizillac felt a surge of contempt for him. "What will you say about all this to his wife?"

"I – I do not know."

"No. Well, I will come to your house with you, and I will speak to her – provided that you now tell me everything about your friendship with Blake."

The carriage took another fifteen minutes to reach the Rue Marbeuf. It was long enough for Rougemont to give the other man an account of his knowledge of Franklin Blake, an account which Boizillac had little doubt was partial, but which was at least consistent in portraying the Englishman as fond of wine, women and song, but devoid of any trait of violence towards his fellow human beings.

"And what did you expect would happen tonight, between the Englishman and the woman in the *auberge*?"

Rougemont was silent for a second or two. "I thought that he would offer her money, and that would be an end of it."

Boizillac felt sure that the other man was holding information back. He had not explained why he had abandoned Blake at the *auberge*: and he had ignored the question about his contact with the other drinker who left just before he did. Boizillac felt he needed to find out more about this unreliable host to his English visitors; and the best way of doing so could well be to enter his house and speak to the Englishman's wife.

They arrived, and both stepped down from the carriage. Moving tentatively, Rougemont went first. Guillaume opened the door to them and took their coats. "Mrs Blake is in the drawing-room," he said.

They went up the stairs. Rougemont opened the door and went in, while Boizillac paused.

Rachel Blake and her maid-servant were sitting in the arm-chairs. At the sight of Rougemont, Penelope stood up and positioned herself behind her mistress, who asked: "Lewis? Is Franklin with you?"

By way of answer, Rougemont beckoned to Boizillac to enter the room. "This is Captain Boizillac, of the Paris police."

Rachel's expression darkened. "The police?"

Boizillac could speak some English, but his uncertain use of the language was made worse by his awareness of a strong resemblance between Rachel Blake and Laure. "Good evening, Mrs Blake. You know where your husband went tonight?"

Rachel's cheeks flushed. "I know that he was going to a tavern, although I do not know its address. Tell me, what has happened to my husband?"

"He has been arrested."

She jumped to her feet. "Arrested? Why?"

"A woman was attacked. Mr Blake was found with her."

"Attacked? What has become of her?"

"The attack was - fatal."

"There must have been a mistake!" The alarm in her voice rang through the room. "What has Franklin said about this?"

"He has said nothing. He was too drunk."

She shook her head repeatedly. "No, no, this cannot be true. Lewis?" But Rougemont returned her gaze in silence. "Lewis, were you not with him when this happened?"

"I – I went with him to the tavern, but he left me to go into a private room with – the woman who was attacked."

"And this woman – was she the actress?"

"You knew that your husband intended to meet Suzanne Pâquerette?" Boizillac asked, remembering the details that Rougemont had given him during their coach ride.

Rachel's voice had become cold now. "My husband explained everything to me. How he had known this woman when he was last in Paris, and how she had written to him this week, seeking to blackmail him. He went to the tavern tonight to talk sense to her and perhaps even to assist her financially. He did not go there to attack her." Her eyes glittered with indignation. "Lewis, you cannot believe that Franklin did this."

"No, I do not," Rougemont said, with desperate sincerity. "I should not have allowed us to be separated. I cannot understand what happened." He hung his head.

The Englishwoman turned to the other man. "Captain Boizillac, where is my husband now?"

"I expect that Inspector Graize has taken him to the Dépôt de la Préfecture – the cells for confining anyone who has just been arrested."

"Who is Inspector Graize? Is he your superior officer?"

"It is difficult to explain, Mrs Blake, but it was Inspector Graize who arrested your husband at the tavern. I was there for another reason, but it seemed useful to me to accompany Monsieur Rougemont when he came back here." He felt that he was being studied closely by the young Englishwoman.

"Can I visit my husband in prison?"

"Tomorrow, yes. Not tonight – visits are not possible at night."

There were a few moments of silence, while Rachel considered his words, and mastered her agitation. She spoke first to Rougemont. "Lewis, I am sorry that your house has been inconvenienced by this disturbance. I trust, however, that I and my maid-servant may continue to enjoy your hospitality for at least another day, until we can see more clearly what will befall Franklin." Rougemont gave her that assurance.

She turned to the other man. "Captain Boizillac, in coming here tonight, it cannot have been your intention to explain these events to the wife of the man whom you saw arrested. But you have indeed done so, and I thank you for it. I have a request to make of you, and I hope that you will not think it too importunate.

"I have little knowledge of the ways of your country, and none of its system of justice. Would you be able to guide me to the prison where my husband is being held – the Dépôt? - tomorrow, and do what you can to ensure that I obtain an interview with him?"

It was clear to Boizillac that Rougemont, though her host, was seen by the Englishwoman as an unreliable ally; he sensed that, with her husband imprisoned and her host disqualified, she knew no-one else in the city who could help her in her present situation. He bowed his head briefly. "I shall return here by ten o'clock tomorrow morning, Mrs Blake."

"Thank you." The words were spoken firmly, but there were tears in her eyes. "Would you excuse me, Captain Boizillac, Lewis? I shall retire now." The two men nodded to her. Boizillac noticed how, almost absent-mindedly, the Englishwoman took the hand of her servant as they left the room.

The young police officer took his leave as well, reminding Rougemont that he would be back in little more than twelve hours.

Chapter Five
Thursday 16 September 1852 – Paris - Rue de Calais

Ledouin had fallen asleep in his hotel puzzling over what had happened at the *Auberge des Dunes*. There was little chance that Rougemont had any idea: he would speak to him later. But, as he readied himself for the new day, Ledouin decided that he needed to talk to Ricord, the tavern-owner. As the city came to life, he made his way to the Rue de Calais.

Approaching from the Rue Grange, he walked the length of the street to the Rue des Vinaigriers, paused, and re-traced his steps. There was no sign of the previous night's excitement: if the local residents knew of the assault on La Pâquerette and the arrest of Franklin Blake, they kept it to themselves as they went about their business. The *Auberge des Dunes* was closed; but Ledouin knew from his previous visits that Ricord opened the tavern's doors only after eleven in the morning.

In other circumstances, Ledouin would have bided his time. But today he had no wish to spend two hours skulking in doorways; there was a light rain falling, and he had other things to do as the day wore on. He stepped up to the tavern, rattled the handle to no effect, and knocked firmly on the door – once, twice, and a third time.

A window above his head scraped open and Ricord looked down at him. "What the hell do you want?"

"Ten minutes' conversation." Ledouin spoke calmly.

The tavern-keeper snorted. "D'you think I run a literary *salon*? Leave me alone." He began to shut the window again.

The investigation agent rattled the door-handle for several seconds, then spoke again. "Just ten minutes, Monsieur Ricord. Or would you prefer that I make a nuisance of myself down here for that long?"

There was an unintelligible curse from the first floor and the window slammed shut. A minute later, Ricord unlocked the door and confronted his visitor. "I thought we'd finished our business." Ledouin went inside and sat at a table. The tavern-keeper quickly locked the door again, then stood with arms crossed. "Don't expect me to bring you a drink."

"Monsieur Ricord, you remember the plan that we agreed. Mademoiselle Pâquerette would come here and meet Mister Blake. She would refuse any offer that he made her, of money or anything else, and she would denounce him in front of everyone in your tavern, and then leave to speak ill of him to others. But instead, here in your tavern, she was done to death, Mister Blake was arrested as her attacker, and now he is locked up in prison." He waited to see if the other man commented, but Ricord's mouth remained closed. "What happened, Monsieur Ricord?"

"The Englishman drank too much."

"Well, I have learnt a great deal about Franklin Blake in recent months. I can believe that he is attracted to women of the *demi-monde*, like Mademoiselle Pâquerette. I can believe that he enjoys wine so much that he sometimes drinks more than he should. But I cannot believe that, sober or drunk, he would ever attack a woman. Mister Blake is a gentleman." Ricord shrugged his shoulders and said nothing. "Why did you send for Alfred Graize last night?"

The Frenchman took a few seconds to reply. "He deals with crime. I thought I needed him."

"Because a man and a woman were drinking together in your private room?"

"You saw what happened. There was a crime. Graize needed to deal with it." Ricord's voice rose again. "You wanted to destroy the Englishman's reputation. Well, you've got what you wanted. Now leave me alone." He opened the door again, pointedly.

"I wanted Mister Blake's reputation to be ruined. But I did not want Mademoiselle Pâquerette to come to harm." Ledouin stood up. "If you have no more to say to me, Monsieur Ricord, I shall leave. I must seek answers to my questions from others." He stepped back out into the street: the tavern-door banged shut at his back.

It was here in the street the night before that Ledouin had spoken briefly to Rougemont, only to find that the Frenchman was as surprised by events as he was, and considerably more discountenanced. It had not escaped Ledouin's attention that the police captain – Boizillac, was it? - who suddenly appeared on the scene had climbed aboard Rougemont's coach. He wanted to know what had transpired between the two of them, but caution was of the essence.

Ledouin made his way across the city to the Rue Marbeuf and found a discreet corner from where he could watch the rented house. His surveillance was soon rewarded when he saw a coach arrive, Boizillac get down from it, be admitted to the house, and then re-emerge within minutes in the company of two figures – Rougemont, and the young wife of Franklin Blake. The coach drove off with the two others in it, while Rougemont turned on his heel and went back inside.

The investigation agent met with no warmer a welcome here than he had done at the *Auberge des Dunes*. He was let in by Guillaume, and climbed the stairs to the first floor. As he went into the drawing-room, he surprised Rougemont standing by the windows. The Frenchman hurriedly put something into his pocket, then sat down heavily in one of the chairs, groaning quietly.

"Good morning," said Ledouin. He crossed the room, so that he could look alternately at Rougemont and the street below. "Has Mrs Blake gone to see her husband?"

"Are you watching this house all the time?" There was a weariness about the Frenchman. "Yes. She asked the police captain – Boizillac - to accompany her."

"She didn't ask you to go with her?"

"She made the request yesterday night, and her mind was unchanged this morning." There was a tone of defiance in his voice, pushing back against any implication that he should have stepped up to the task of joining Rachel.

"No matter. Her absence makes it easier for us to converse." He looked out and saw that the rain was falling heavily now. Poor weather for a prison visit, he thought to himself. "Monsieur Rougemont, I know that you and Captain Boizillac travelled back here together last night. Would you be good enough to tell me exactly what you said to him?"

"I didn't tell him it was you who dragged me out of my quiet existence in the provinces and set me up in this house and gave me this impossible role to act!" It was flung at Ledouin as an accusation. The investigation agent remembered the alacrity with which the Frenchman had received his regular payments, and the preening eagerness with which he had taken up residence in the Rue Marbeuf. But it was not constancy of character which had led Ledouin to make use of him – quite the reverse. After a few seconds, Rougemont resumed in a calmer tone. "I told him about the time that Blake and I spent together four or five years ago, and about his old liaison with the actress. And I told him that she had threatened to expose it all, and that he went to the *Auberge des Dunes* to try and talk her out of it."

"And you didn't say that it was in Mr Blake's mind to attack the actress?"

Rougemont flared up again, momentarily. "Of course not. I said that I expected him to buy her silence with money, not to do anything else. That was never his way."

Ledouin studied him for a few seconds. "I am obliged to you, Monsieur Rougemont, for providing as much intelligence to the captain of police as it was right for him to receive, without burdening him with unnecessary details." He smiled at the other man, whose face was still shadowed by resentment. Ledouin had little time for Rougemont's tendency to self-pity, but there were other traits to him which prompted some sympathy in the investigation agent. "And I agree with you about Mister Franklin Blake. He is not a violent man. And yet Mademoiselle Pâquerette was attacked. It is difficult to make sense of it all, isn't it?"

There was silence for a few moments. Then Rougemont spoke, haltingly. "You must understand. I told Boizillac that I couldn't imagine Blake attacking the woman, and I gave Mrs Blake my wholehearted support in rejecting the idea. But – I have turned this over in my mind since last night, and – I see no other explanation." He paused. "Blake was reeking of wine. So much wine must have changed him, turned him into someone different. This woman – La Pâquerette – was threatening to ruin him. He must have attacked her, without knowing what he was doing."

Was it possible? Ledouin wondered. Unlike the Frenchman, he knew all the history of Blake's complicity in the theft of the Moonstone four years before. Could the wine he drank in the tavern have acted as another opiate, dulling his normal senses so that criminal impulses took over? "Do you believe that?" he asked.

Rougemont's head slumped. "I am compelled to."

There was nothing more to discuss. "I shall leave you now, Monsieur Rougemont. I acknowledge that your role here has become much more difficult, but I would ask you to continue in it. Afford such comfort and hospitality to Mrs Blake as you can, until the fate of her husband becomes clearer. I must return to London, to let my client know how matters have turned out. But rest assured that I shall communicate again with you in a matter of days."

***

Before making his way to the Rue Marbeuf, Boizillac had gone to the Dépôt de la Préfecture, and confirmed that Franklin Blake had spent the night there. The Englishman had clearly still had money on him when he was arrested; the second floor of the Dépôt had a series of private cells – *prisons de pistole* – and Blake was shut up in one of these.

Several minutes passed in silence after Mrs Blake joined him in his carriage and they rode towards the heart of the city, silence broken only by the sound of rain falling on the vehicle's roof. It startled Boizillac when the young woman suddenly spoke. "I have never visited a prison before, Captain Boizillac. What manner of place should I expect?" The effort that she took to keep her voice calm was only too audible.

"It is not an agreeable place, Madame Blake. The people who are held in prisons are also, usually, not agreeable."

"And is my husband accommodated alongside such people?"

"No, not at the Dépôt. He is held in a room on his own."

"Why so? Is that because he is English?"

"No, Madame Blake, it is because he has paid for the room."

She was silent again for some time. Boizillac looked out and saw that they were riding alongside the Seine, a great mass of water that flowed sluggishly on, with grey indifference to the plight of the thousands of people in the streets and houses around it. A sob escaped from the woman next to him. "Ah Franklin, what have you done!" She dabbed at her eyes, then breathed deeply. "Forgive me, Captain Boizillac, I resolved not to succumb to my feelings, and now I have done so. It will not happen again."

"Madame Blake, you do not need to seek my forgiveness --"

"Thank you." She cut across him. "Let me rather seek practical information from you. Shall I be able to meet my husband in this cell in which he is accommodated?"

"It is normal for such meetings to take place in the *parloir*, a hall in which a prisoner sits in a stall with a grating at one end, which communicates with a second stall in which the visitor sits."

"But that is like nothing so much as gazing upon a wild animal in captivity!"

"You must understand, Madame Blake, that some prisoners are desperate, and would take any chance to escape. But I hope that you may be permitted to speak to your husband in his room. I shall do what I can to make this possible."

"And will you of necessity remain with us throughout our interview?"

He paused. "As you say, Madame, that will be a necessity."

Rachel reflected for a few moments. "Then may I ask, Captain Boizillac, that, whatever my husband and I say to one another during our meeting, you believe my assurance that Franklin and I are one heart and one soul, and that nothing that has happened in this city can ever make us otherwise."

By way of acknowledgement, Boizillac inclined his head. It was impossible to doubt the sincerity of the Englishwoman: how credible, though, would her husband prove?

They arrived at the Dépôt. Boizillac stepped down from the carriage first, and waited for his companion to follow. He saw how she paused before alighting, looking at the scene before her. Her gaze was fixed: the three-storey prison, built with great blocks of rough-hewn stone, punctuated by narrow windows barred by rusting metal, and covered now with a green-tinged patina of trickling rain-water, gave off an air of menace, and seemed to her like some great reptile squatting in river-mud. She gathered her cape more tightly around her, and descended carefully to the street.

Going ahead, he went up to the gate that closed the entrance and spoke through a hatch at eye-level. The guard on the other side heard him out, looked both Boizillac and Rachel up and down, and unbolted the gate. They went through: the gate was immediately shut again.

It was very dark. There were burning candles fixed to the wall on either side of the entrance, but their light reached no more than a few feet. Further along on the ground floor, behind another barrier of grating, other candles showed a dozen or more women, dressed in costumes ranging from cheap ball-gowns to simple smocks. They sat, or lay, on benches attached to the walls. One of them saw the new arrivals and shouted: "Welcome to the sisterhood of the Palace, sweetheart!"

"Who are these people?" Rachel asked.

"Street-walkers," Boizillac replied. Seeing a lack of understanding, he added: "They go with men for money. If they cause a disturbance, they are brought here and released again after half a day."

"And then?" she asked. "Do they simply go back to walking the streets?" He nodded. She turned her eyes away from the women. "Can we find my husband?"

There was a staircase to their left, which they now climbed. The first floor held the private cells for women; men were on the floor above that. The landing was occupied by another guard, a hulk of a man with grey hair, a double chin and a paunch, who sat hunched over a table on which were placed a sheaf of papers, a wooden club, a large bunch of keys, scraps of bread and meat and a pitcher of water.

"We want to talk to Mr Franklin Blake," Boizillac said to the guard, who stared sullenly at him. "He was brought here last night by Inspector Graize."

"Oh, him. The English milord who was drunk as a skunk." His chubby hands shuffled the papers on the table. Boizillac suspected that this was for form's sake; he doubted that the man could read. "He's in cell number seven. Is this his wife?" The younger man nodded. "She deserves better. And you?"

"Captain Boizillac, of the Sûreté."

It was as if someone had cracked a whip. The guard got to his feet, heavily but without further delay. "Dutrait, captain." He picked up the keys. "Cell number seven." He walked several paces and then turned again to Boizillac. "I gave him some food this morning, but he refused it. Still the worse for wear from last night." He mimicked the action of a drinker. "Food was perfectly good, mind you. I couldn't let it go to waste, could I?" He patted his stomach. "If he wants anything now, I can send out for it. Will you stay in there with them?" Boizillac nodded. "Good. Here you are then." He put a key in the lock of a door marked with a white 7, turned it with some effort, and waved them inside. "Have to lock up behind you. Shout when you need me."

It was a small enough room, perhaps five paces deep, and no wider than the rough wooden bed that was fixed to the outer wall. There was otherwise one stern chair and a half-sized table; a crucifix hung on the side-wall. Though the window above the bed was narrow and intersected by metal bars, its opening made the room markedly lighter than the rest of the building's interior; and it showed the figure lying on the bed, who now sat upright and looked towards the door.

Boizillac entered first. "Who are you?" Blake asked. The Frenchman stood to one side; his companion came in. "Rachel? Rachel!" He jumped up and hurried to hold her.

Their embrace lasted several seconds. Then the Englishwoman stepped back. "Franklin, this is a dreadful place. I have heard from others why you have been brought here. But you must tell me yourself what happened last night."

"That is what I most desire, Rachel. But --" he paused and looked at the third person in the room, "who is this man?"

"He is Captain Boizillac, of the Paris police. He came to our lodgings last night, with Monsieur Rougemont, and explained that you had been arrested. At my request, he accompanied me today to assist me in visiting you. I am greatly in his debt."

"Why then, so am I. I thank you most sincerely, Captain. You understand English?" Boizillac nodded. "Could you leave me alone with my wife?"

"I regret that I cannot, Monsieur Blake. But, if you will allow me, I shall spend my time here at the window, looking at what I can see of Paris. Please ignore me."

Rachel grasped Blake's hands. "Captain Boizillac warned me that he would have to remain with us. Give no more thought to it, Franklin. We have little enough time for this interview." She sat on the chair; her hands were still entwined with those of her husband, who stood above her, his back to the Frenchman. "You look pale, Franklin. Are you ill?"

"No, not ill, save that I am still recovering from the state of intoxication which overtook me last night. Do not reproach me for that, Rachel. Though I went to a tavern, I had no mind to drink. But when I sat down with that woman, we were served wine, and she insisted that I drank with her if we were to talk matters through. I recall drinking one glass only - yet my memory must deceive me, for one glass would never have pitched me into the abyss in which I found myself."

"You know that your clothes are drenched with the smell of wine. None of this can be the work of one glass."

Blake's head dropped momentarily. "No, indeed."

"I shall ensure that you have fresh clothes before the end of the day." She looked at him intensely. "And the woman, Franklin?" She paused. "You spoke with her?"

"Why yes. I told her that I wanted nothing more to do with her."

"But how harshly did you deal with her?"

"I spoke clearly. She can have been in no doubt."

"Franklin, did you attack the woman? Did the wine cloud your mind - did anger overmaster you so that you -- laid your hands on her?"

"No!" It was a defiant shout. "You cannot believe that of me! I have no memory of drinking myself to intoxication - but even a drugged memory must retain knowledge of such a foul act of violence, and my memory is clear of it."

There was a long silence, while the two looked deep into each other's eyes. Both recalled the night some four years earlier, when the Moonstone had been stolen from Rachel's bedroom, a theft committed by an unknowing perpetrator who passed the following twelve months in ignorance of his action. By Blake himself. Finally Rachel spoke. "No, I do not believe it of you, Franklin. And yet, unless a truer explanation of the crime is offered, we must fear that others will assume that you are capable of such an act. We must fear, dear heart, that your return to England and your family will be long delayed."

"It cannot, it must not be! Surely the police of Paris must see the truth of my innocence!"

"You must contain yourself, Franklin. You forget that Captain Boizillac is with us."

The Englishman turned round. "I had forgotten, for the moment. But perhaps I may be permitted to ask Monsieur Boizillac a question."

Boizillac faced him. "Of course, Mister Blake."

"My question is this. As a gentleman, who has lived a life free of violence and wrong-doing, must I labour under the suspicion that I attacked Mademoiselle Pâquerette? Is not my character evidence enough that I have been wrongly arrested?"

The Frenchman paused before replying. "I am sorry that you find yourself here, Mister Blake. I have heard the same description of your character from Monsieur Rougemont, and from your wife."

He looked from husband to wife, and saw the fevered hope in the eyes of Blake countered by the anxiety on Rachel's face. "But as to evidence - you were found in the same room as the victim of an attack, a woman who was threatening you with public disgrace, and your person shows all the signs of dishonourable conduct." Blake's face was bruised, his shirt torn, his coat stained by wine. "Any man arrested on the basis of such evidence must expect to go to trial."

"To trial?" Blake repeated. "I - I shall stand trial here?"

"I am sorry."

Blake's energy left him suddenly. Turning back to his wife, he fell to his knees on the floor in front of her. "Forgive me, Rachel, my dearest. How happy we were when we arrived in Paris, and how wretched we are now. Forgive me!" He hung his head.

"Listen to me, Franklin." His wife's voice was urgent and forceful. "This is a misfortune which no-one could have foreseen. But we have conquered adversity before, you and I. We must do so again. We must prepare ourselves to prove your innocence. I know nothing of French law, or French lawyers. But we can rely on Mr Bruff, of Gray's Inn Square. His legal mind helped us before, and it can do so again. I am resolved to travel back to London at the earliest opportunity, and engage Mr Bruff in the matter."

"You will leave me in Paris?"

"You must see that I have to, Franklin, but I shall return with Mr Bruff as soon as he and I are able."

Hope crept back into Blake's voice. "Yes, yes, the estimable Bruff will know what to do. Oh Rachel, what a marvel you are! Thank you, my dearest."

"Then, Franklin, I had best go now and make arrangements. Captain Boizillac?" The Frenchman went to the door and called out. Dutrait arrived quickly, and unlocked. Boizillac stepped outside and spoke in a low tone with the guard for a minute or so, allowing Rachel to take her leave of Blake in private. She emerged; the cell was locked again; she rested her hand briefly on the closed door, then hurried down the stairs and out of the building, with Boizillac behind her.

He flagged down a carriage for her. "You will stay here?" she asked, after climbing into it.

"I have other duties, Madame Blake."

"Then, thank you again." She shut the carriage door and spoke through the window. "I am sure that my husband is innocent, but I see that there is much for me to do to persuade the rest of the world of that - first in London and then back here in Paris. We may meet again when I return. *Au revoir*, Captain Boizillac." And she was gone.

He stood for a while, watching the carriage disappear, not noticing the rain soaking through the shoulders of his greatcoat. If there was any hope for the Englishman, it rested with her; there was no doubting her determination; but nor was there any way to overlook the evidence that he had described to Blake in his cell.

He was jolted out of his reflections when he heard his name barked at him from the direction of the Dépôt. The man strode rapidly over to him: a broad-brimmed hat covered his baldness, but there was no mistaking the sombre beard, or hostile intent. "So you are here as well?"

"Good day to you, Graize," Boizillac countered. "I have just accompanied the wife of the Englishman on a visit to her husband."

Graize's eyes glared at him from under his hat. "What is the Englishman, or his wife, to you?"

"I knew neither of them before last night. But his wife asked me to go with her, and I did so."

"You saw the man when you stumbled into the tavern last night. How did you meet his wife?"

The other man's hectoring manner was getting under Boizillac's skin. "One of the other drinkers in the tavern was a friend of Blake. Louis Rougemont. Blake and his wife were staying in Rougemont's house here in Paris. I followed Rougemont home last night." He paused and added. "I thought it might be helpful to hear what he had to say about Blake's assignation in the tavern. You may wish to know what he said."

Graize drew breath before answering. "It may be chivalry that prompted you to come here with the Englishman's wife, Boizillac, or you may have some other motive. At all events, the fate of her husband rests in my hands, and I need no assistance from you. Don't waste your breath on repeating whatever stories you heard from this Rougemont. The Englishman was found *in flagrante delicto*, and justice will be done."

"But the man Blake --"

Graize snatched his hat from his head: the fierceness of his eyes was unmistakable. "You have no more to say in this case, Boizillac. Go about your own business, and leave mine to me." He wiped the rain from the top of his head, pulled his hat back on, and strode away, into the Dépôt.

Once again, Boizillac had failed to ask Graize about Cotte; this time, it was clear to the younger man that the chance to do so was unlikely to arise. He wondered whether Graize's hostility was personal to him alone, whether there was something about his own manner which irritated Graize; but Taillefer had said that he would try and walk all over him if their paths crossed, and Boizillac could almost feel the imprints of Graize's boots on his back.

And now he could feel the rain through his coat. He hurried away from the Dépôt; it was true, he had his own business to attend to, and it was time for him to do so.

Chapter Six

Friday 17 September 1852 – London - Bethnal Green Cut

Sequestered in his garret, Luker found it a relief to throw off the French persona that he had inhabited for most of the week: no more need to hold his head high and his shoulders back, or to lift his natural frown into an expression of open self-confidence. He had returned to London late the night before, and leaving behind the sordid shock of the last few days in Paris felt like losing a millstone from around his neck.

He would have to go back, of course. But first of all, he would have to explain events to his client. Mr Blake-Hater had continued to withhold his real name from Luker, but had told him that, if he needed to be in touch urgently, he could leave a message - "which you should address to Mr John Yorkshire" - with one of the reception clerks at the finance-house near Threadneedle Street. Luker had done so, first thing that morning. Now he sat in his own office, awaiting his client's arrival. He had suggested noon: as the clock approached midday, he heard the sound of footsteps climbing the stairs.

Luker met his client on the landing and ushered him through to the inner sanctum.

There were no initial pleasantries. "So? Was the trap sprung? Has Blake met with his disgrace?"

"He has, but not in the way that was planned."

"What's that? What has happened, then?"

"On Wednesday of this week, he went to the tavern where the French actress told him to meet her. I had agreed with her on the role that she would play - just as I had arranged matters with Monsieur Rougemont, who accommodated Mr Blake and his wife during their stay in Paris - and with Monsieur Ricord, the tavern-keeper."

"Aye, I recall all these details, and the payments that they cost."

"As you say, sir. All the preparations had been made. The actress was to confront Mr Blake in the tavern and then blacken his name publicly. But it did not come to that."

"What?" The older man's face began to redden.

"Allow me to finish, sir. It did not come to that because, an hour or so after Mr Blake and the actress withdrew to a private room, we heard confused sounds from within, the door was forced open, and Mademoiselle Pâquerette could be seen, fallen to the floor, and strangled dead."

114

"In God's name! And Blake?"

"He was in the same room, rendered insensate by too much wine."

"Blake had done this harm to the woman?"

"He had fallen on top of her. There was no-one else in the room. Blake was arrested by the French police and is now detained in a prison in Paris."

There was silence in the darkened room. Then the client spoke again, more slowly. "Blake arrested for the murder of a Frenchwoman, of questionable virtue, in a lowly Parisian tavern." He shook his head, almost disbelievingly. "Well, Luker, I'll not credit you with foreseeing this outcome. But you brought the wolf and the lamb together. It is no surprise if the lamb's flesh has been torn asunder. No surprise to me." There was a look of contentment on his face.

"You will appreciate, sir, that Mr Blake's guilt has yet to be proven, through a process of trial."

"From what you tell me, there can be little doubt that he is the guilty party. And at all events, the circumstances of his discovery will leave a lasting stain on his character. I congratulate you, Mr Luker. This is a consummation greatly to be welcomed."

Though he kept his reaction hidden, Luker felt discomfited by these congratulations. He had seen the broken figure of Suzanne Pâquerette, and he was unhappy to think that it had been his scheming that brought her to this ordeal. Would Mr Blake-Hater have been less exultant if he too had seen the beaten woman? It was not obvious that he would. But there was another concern that Luker had to raise. "I fear, however, that there may be a complication."

"Speak up then. What complication?"

"Monsieur Rougemont."

"The fellow who's spent the summer in some fine Parisian villa paid for by my money?"

Luker nodded. "I can assure you that his performance as host to Mr Blake and his wife was exemplary. But --
"

"Go on, man."

"Monsieur Rougemont was no less shaken by Mr Blake's apparent attack on Mademoiselle Pâquerette than I. We both left the tavern once the scene in the private room had been revealed. But, while I returned to my hotel unchallenged, Monsieur Rougemont's departure was observed by an officer of the Paris police who questioned him closely about Mr Blake, and his relationship with the actress."

"Did he, indeed? And what did Rougemont say?"

"Nothing about my arrangement with him. I pressed him on this, and I believe his assurances. But Monsieur

Rougemont is not the strongest of characters, and I fear that I cannot permanently rely on his discretion."

"I grow concerned, Luker. Have you a remedy?"

"I have, sir. And that is what I particularly wish to discuss with you." Luker had thought this over on his journey back to England. "It will take some time for the French authorities to resolve Mr Blake's fate. If Monsieur Rougemont were absent from Paris for that duration, there would be no further possibility for the police to question him and perhaps hear some indiscretion from him."

"Do I need to dig into my pockets again, Luker?"

"I had in mind to propose that Monsieur Rougemont might spend the next month or so in Italy. I am confident that he would be drawn to the delights of that country. And the expenditure required would be in part offset by ending the lease on the Paris house where he is now accommodated."

"You consider this necessary?"

"He needs to be distracted from the shock of the last few days, and placed out of the way of further inquiry."

The client reached inside his coat and brought out an envelope, which he placed on the table. "That is a good deal of money, Luker. I had some inkling that it might be needed. Use it to bring this affair to a proper conclusion. I shall wish you to account for it in due course, but let us not draw up columns and write down figures now. You must return to Paris, of course. When do you go?"

"With your approval, sir, tomorrow."

"Good." The old man got to his feet, and paused. "Blake is in prison. What has become of his wife?"

"She was still lodging at Monsieur Rougemont's house when I left, sir. Whether she will choose to stay in Paris while Mr Blake's fate is decided, or else come back to London, I cannot say."

"Once Rougemont leaves for Italy, she cannot stay in that house, can she?"

"Not unless you wish me to make some other arrangements, sir."

"I do not. She must make what shift she can." He buttoned up his coat and walked to the stairs. "You have done well, Luker. The wolf has shown his teeth. Now let him be caged." He left.

Alone again, Luker assessed the contents of the envelope which the client had given him. If money could talk, he thought, this amount would shout out, proclaiming loudly how much the man hated Mr Blake. Luker turned his thoughts to planning his next moves.

***

Saturday 18 September 1852 - London - Gray's Inn

Matthew Bruff had handled the legal affairs of the Verinder family for many years. He had been of particular help to Rachel Verinder, as she then was, four years before, when she had been given the Moonstone and seen it stolen, and when she had been briefly, and unhappily, engaged to Godfrey Ablewhite. He remained on close terms with Rachel and her husband after their marriage, but, with issues relating to inheritance and income long settled, it was some time since he had seen either of them.

It was a surprise to him then, seated in his Gray's Inn office that Saturday morning, reviewing the week's correspondence, when his clerk knocked, looked in and said: "Mrs Rachel Blake would like to speak to you, sir."

The papers that were in his hand dropped on to the desk. He put his spectacles next to them and, patting down the dishevelled strands of grey hair on his head, he went across to the door. He saw the young woman, dressed as demurely as ever, waiting in the outer room. "Rachel. How unexpected." The cast of her face conveyed to him that this was not a social call. "Is all well? Please, come in, and sit down." She went through and took a chair. He nodded to his clerk and shut the door.

Even as he took his seat, Rachel leaned forward on her chair, and spoke urgently. "Mr Bruff, I hope that it is not inconvenient that I have come here unannounced. I was not sure that you would be here. I am glad that you are. But all is not well. Franklin and I travelled to Paris last week. On our second day there, he was arrested for assaulting a Frenchwoman. He now sits in a Parisian prison, awaiting trial. We agreed that I should come back to London and seek your advice."

Her words drove the smile of welcome from Bruff's face. "Franklin arrested?" She nodded. "May I ask who this Frenchwoman was?"

Rachel held her gaze steady. "You know that, in the years before we were married, Franklin led an existence that was occasionally frivolous. He spent some time in Paris, and the woman was one of his companions from that period."

"But why did he wish to renew their connection?"

"He had no such wish. But, as fate would have it, the woman recognised Franklin when he and I were seeing the sights of Paris. She discovered where we were staying and sent him a letter, demanding a meeting, and threatening public disgrace otherwise. Franklin and I agreed that he should see her."

"You did not go with him?"

"That seemed inappropriate." The word was carefully chosen. "But our host in Paris, Monsieur Rougemont, accompanied Franklin, to the tavern appointed for the meeting." She paused; Bruff waited. "And it was there that the woman was attacked, and Franklin was discovered in circumstances that, to all but those who know him well, suggested that he was her assailant."

"Circumstances?"

"They were in a private room at the tavern. Franklin was intoxicated, his clothes marked with wine, his face bruised. The woman had been strangled."

"And Franklin was apprehended?"

"The police arrested him on the spot, and confined him in the prison of the Prefecture. I visited him there two days ago, and we resolved that I should call on you with all urgency."

Bruff got up from his desk. For some moments he walked around his office, taking a thick volume in his hand, then putting it down again. Rachel's eyes never left him. He came and stood near her. "Well, my dear, this is very serious. It would be no small matter to extricate him from such a situation if the attack had taken place in this country. That it occurred in France, and that Franklin is now confined by French justice, makes it a very big matter indeed." He paused. "I take it that there is no doubt in your mind that Franklin is innocent of this crime?"

"None." The reply was instant. "You will have the theft of the Moonstone in your mind. Though Franklin acted then without his own knowledge, he was driven by a protective impulse, a wish to protect me. There is no spark of violence within him, nothing within his character that would lead him to harm another person, even if his mind were clouded by an intoxicant."

"Then I harbour no doubts either." He began to pace the room again. "We should seek to involve our ambassador in Paris in this matter. I shall send a letter without delay - but, though he may make representations to the French Government on Franklin's behalf, it would be unwise to hope too strongly that he might be released without some process of justice." He looked out of his window, at the autumn-tinged trees in the courtyard beyond. "No, the best course of action is for me to travel to Paris and, on your behalf, engage a French advocate to conduct Franklin's defence if, or more probably, when he is required to stand trial." He turned to face Rachel again. "I have had dealings with my French counterparts on occasions, and I am confident that I can find the right man to champion Franklin. It would be unwise to delay in the face of the gravity of the crime for which Franklin was arrested. I shall go on Monday."

"And I shall go with you."

"You are sure of that? Your young child - Julia?"

"She will be well cared for in my absence. I think that she and I can bear with a few more days' separation. Franklin, however --" She left the sentence unfinished.

"Very well. Would you intend to stay with your former host, this Monsieur Rougemont?"

Rachel looked down briefly. "I think not. I am grateful to him for opening his house to us. But, ashamed though I am to say it, I felt that his friendship with

Franklin faltered at the moment of crisis. I have no wish to place any further burden on that connection."

Bruff recognised again the clarity of insight which he had seen in Rachel throughout her life, and which she had inherited from her mother. "In that case, if you allow, I will ensure that we find suitable accommodation. I have previously stayed at the Hotel Bristol, in the Place Vendôme. That should serve."

The young woman got to her feet. "As an old friend of the family, you need no assurance from me, Mr Bruff, of the debt of gratitude that I owe you for this assistance, and for your past help. Please accept my thanks, and those of Franklin."

Bruff bowed his head momentarily. "Well, well, we shall come through this as we came through past misfortune. I shall consult my clerk, and then send a note to you about arrangements on Monday." He guided her to the door. "I wish that we had met again in happier circumstances, but those will arrive."

Rachel said nothing more, and left. The lawyer stood in thought for a few moments, then turned to making plans for the visit to Paris.

Chapter Seven
Sunday 19 September 1852 – Lyon

The procession of the Prince-President had reached France's second city. Lyon had a history of resenting the pre-eminence of Paris in the nation's affairs, and there had been fears that its citizens might not show the same warmth to the capital city's latest master as had been apparent elsewhere. Those fears were unfounded. As Louis-Napoléon rode from the railway station to the Prefecture, he drew cheers from the watching crowds which were just as enthusiastic as those in Bourges, or Orléans. The next day, he would unveil a huge statue of his uncle, the founder of the Bonaparte dynasty, imperially seated astride a powerful horse: at one and the same time, it glorified the past, and foreshadowed the future, the return of the Emperor in the next generation of the family.

Victor de Persigny, his Interior Minister, was still with him, making sure that the preparations for the tour of the provinces, which he had sketched out weeks beforehand, were properly implemented. Their success would prepare the ground for the final transformation of what was nominally still a republic into a new Bonapartist empire.

124

It was the end of a day that had gone well. The Prince-President had spoken well at the reception banquet, praising the city's spirit of independence and industry; and his benevolence had received its echo in the praise, little short of adulation, that the local notables sent in his direction. Louis-Napoléon had retired for the night; but Persigny, his faithful servant, still kept watch, in the ante-chamber to his hotel room where his staff had brought his papers.

There was a knock at the door. Persigny had told his private secretary to go to bed. He admitted the visitor himself.

Charles Rasquin stood in the darkened corridor. Though there was no-one else around, he had struck his usual pose of implied superiority: head and shoulders forced back, chest puffed out, hooded eyes looking with disdain along his prominent nose. His moustache and beard were groomed in the same manner as those of the Prince-President, but extended further to the side and below his chin in a way that verged on caricature. He wore a crumpled frock-coat, that spoke of a past in the army (where he had served without distinction in an earlier decade), and held a battered top-hat and cane in his right hand.

Rasquin had been one of the first "little people" to attach himself to the Bonapartist faction at the time of Louis-Napoléon's election as President of the Second Republic. Most of the other leading supporters of the Prince-President soon lost patience with Rasquin's posturing; Persigny did not, and found by cultivating him that Rasquin had a number of useful contacts around the edges of the criminal underworld. The man had become even more of an asset since Persigny was appointed Interior Minister: for all that the office brought him a wide network of agents and informants, Persigny looked to Rasquin for particular insights into the shadowlands of Paris. Their meetings continued, even though, like this one, they had no official status.

The instant that he saw Persigny, Rasquin's pose changed. As his right hand, with hat and cane, shot out to the side, he bent forward in an exaggerated bow, intoning: "Your servant, Monsieur le Ministre."

"Come in, Rasquin." Persigny took hold of his right arm and pulled the man upright and into his room. He knew of Rasquin's dependence on him; there was no need for it to be demonstrated further. The Minister took a seat behind the desk where his papers lay. His visitor remained standing: he would find it impossible to sit down and thus imply that he was Persigny's equal.

"When did you leave Paris?"

"Yesterday morning, Monsieur."

"A long journey. You have news for me?"

"I do. Some time ago, you were good enough to confide in me in the matter of finding and retrieving artefacts, both redolent of our late, great Emperor, and resonant for our present, glorious Prince-President." Involuntarily, Rasquin twisted the points of his moustache, but said nothing more.

"It is a natural dynastic interest."

"Indeed, Monsieur le Ministre. What could be more natural, or more dynastic?" He shot Persigny a glance of understanding. "I have had some success. It is with particular pride that I recall the acquisition and re-appropriation of an almost pristine set of the 'Five Battles' series of medallions from the Emperor's first Italian campaign. It was my privilege to commit and entrust those medallions to you, Monsieur." Persigny nodded, encouragingly. He knew that Rasquin's sense of privilege had been bolstered by receipt of a healthy payment out of the Minister's special funds, but there was no need to mention that. "And there have been other finds, which I shall not itemise and enumerate now."

"No, there is no need for that. But there is another artefact?"

"An object that bespeaks and evokes the great Emperor's embrace of Egypt." He paused. "An exquisite creation, made of silver and precious stone, in the shape of a bee. It was brought back from the land of the Pharaohs and displayed in the museum of the Louvre, from which it was looted in the riots of 1830. But now it can be returned to its rightful owner - the Emperor's own family."

"If this is true, Rasquin, you have done well indeed. And you have this object?"

"It will have been acquired this very night."

"But not by you?"

"No, Monsieur le Ministre, not by, but for, me. By one of my trusted associates."

"Tell me how you brought this object to light."

"Two days ago, I had word from another associate - a man loyal to the Emperor's cause - that he had been approached by someone seeking to interest him in the purchase of the pendant. I seized the moment and sent a message to this person proposing a meeting that evening, to which he should bring the object for my inspection and verification."

"Did you explain your involvement?"

Rasquin stiffened slightly. "Of that there was no need. My name is inseparable from the cause to which I have devoted myself." Persigny nodded. "We met. He produced the pendant. I could be in no doubt about its importance. I agreed a price for its acquisition, to be completed today."

"The price?"

"One hundred francs."
"I see," Persigny said. "But why did you not complete the transaction yourself?"

"I did not wish to delay the purchase of the object, Monsieur le Ministre, but the outlay of such a sum leaves me in some difficulty. After disbursing one hundred francs, my own funds are depleted and, in truth, exhausted. With the greatest respect, I must turn to you to re-establish my liquidity."

"I see," the Minister repeated. He turned on his chair and unlocked a metal chest that rested on the floor behind him. "Very well, Rasquin, I trust that this pendant is as valuable as you believe. Here is half the amount that is being paid for it. You will receive the other half once the pendant is in my hands."

Rasquin managed to carry out another sweeping bow to Persigny at the same time as he took the money and placed it firmly inside his frock-coat. "It will be with you as soon as I can arrange it."

"Good." He sat down again. "Who is this vendor of the pendant?"

"A young man who seems to have a greater attachment to money than to moral fibre," Rasquin said, with disapproval. "His name is Rougemont."

"Rougemont?" Persigny echoed. He looked through the papers on his desk, and found a report. He read through it for a minute or so: Rasquin stood mute, and alert. "Louis Rougemont?"

"Yes, Monsieur le Ministre."

"You know that the woman Suzanne Pâquerette was murdered this week, and that an Englishman - Blake - was arrested for the murder?"

"Indeed, Monsieur le Ministre. All of Paris knows about it. A shocking crime."

Persigny ignored the comment. "Did you not know that Blake had been staying in Paris in the house of this Louis Rougemont?" The other man's eyes widened; he gave no reply. Persigny held up the report that was on his desk. "He was with Blake when they made their way to the tavern where the murder took place. Blake went to a private room where he was alone with the woman and, when he was discovered with her dead body, Rougemont slipped away, saying nothing to the police agents who arrested Blake. All this happened on Wednesday - and you say that you saw Rougemont two days ago. You saw him on Friday?"

"Friday, correct, Monsieur le Ministre." There was silence as the Minister pondered the connection for a few moments. Then, clearing his throat nervously, Rasquin spoke again. "The tavern." Persigny looked at him. "The *Auberge des Dunes*."

"Where the woman was killed?"

"Indeed." A quick cough. "That was where I met, where I conferred with Rougemont."

Persigny pushed back his chair and jumped to his feet. "Explain yourself!" He saw Rasquin's face tremble with a spasm of fear. The man was lost for words. Persigny gathered himself, and went on more calmly. "I have no reason to criticise you, Rasquin. I know that you have used that tavern before. But did Rougemont show no signs of concern at returning to the place, only

130

forty-eight hours after the murder? Did he say nothing that revealed his involvement with Blake?"

"No indeed, Monsieur le Ministre. Though --" he paused, consulting his memory. "We used the private room for our discussion, and I recollect now that Rougemont's mind was not always on the subject of our meeting. At times I found it difficult to catch his eye, for he seemed more interested in directing his gaze here, there and everywhere around the room."

"But he said nothing about the crime that had been committed there?"

"No, Monsieur. Had he done so, I would assuredly report it to you."

"I know, Rasquin. And so he showed you this Egyptian pendant, you confirmed your wish to purchase it from him, and the two of you agreed that payment would be made, and the pendant handed over, today, with the transaction handled between Rougemont on the one side and your associate on the other?"

"Monsieur le Ministre has precisely summarised the outcome of the meeting."

"And the time and place of the transaction?"

"Earlier this evening, Rougemont was to wait outside the entrance to the Jardin Marbeuf, to be collected by my associate in a carriage. In such fashion, the interchange of pendant and payment would be seen by no-one."

131

Persigny walked round the desk and rested his arm on the other man's shoulders. "You have served me well, Rasquin. I shall send you word once I return to the capital, and I shall be pleased if you will waste no time in bringing this pendant to me." He looked at the clock in the room. "It is late now. Have you a berth for the night?"

Rasquin stood to attention. "An old soldier can sleep on any patch of earth, so long as no enemy stands on it."

"Can you make yourself comfortable in this ante-chamber?"

"Of course, Monsieur!"

"Then settle down here. I shall retire to my own room. Mind, it would be as well if you took your leave at sunrise." He locked his papers away in the one of the desk-drawers, picked up the chest from the floor, nodded again at Rasquin, and withdrew into his bed-room.

The other man stood for several minutes, head and shoulders tilted backwards, breathing deeply to inhale the air that was infused with Ministerial power. There was a sofa in the corner of the ante-chamber. Taking off his boots, he set them down carefully on the carpet alongside his hat and cane; unbuttoned his frock-coat and, lying down, spread it over him as a cover; and fell asleep, dreaming of pendants, palaces and the smiling face of the Emperor-to-be.

Sunday 19 September - Paris - Rue Marbeuf

Contrary to the plan that he had agreed with his client, Luker was not able to travel from London on Saturday. Soon after seeing Mr Blake-Hater, the investigation agent felt chilled to his bones, and was obliged to spend twenty-four hours in bed, swaddled in blankets, drinking a hot toddy of tea and gin, and struggling fitfully against a rheumatic attack. A day's rest restored him. He travelled to Paris on Sunday, and announced himself at the house in Rue Marbeuf soon after eight in the evening. He was too late.

Rougemont had his own plan. On their way to the tavern the previous Wednesday, he had persuaded Blake to hand him back the Egyptian pendant. The Englishman had it on his person, in case he needed to offer it to Suzanne Pâquerette; but Rougemont's last-minute pleading for its return to him, as a memento of his father, changed Blake's mind in his favour. It meant that Rougemont had an asset that he could trade for money; and he had decided to use that money to quit Paris and the charade of the Rue Marbeuf. He was not to know that Luker intended to make him a similar offer, and one that would have served him far better.

When he heard from the intermediary on the Friday morning that he could meet Rasquin that evening, but in the *Auberge des Dunes*, he was momentarily brought up short. It seemed an ill omen, to negotiate the sale of the pendant in the very place where the woman had been killed. But two things decided him to go ahead. If this was the tavern where Rasquin chose to conduct

133

business, and where the man could be expected to offer him a good price for the pendant, Rougemont was prepared to suppress his concern about the place. And, with one part of his mind, he felt drawn to see the tavern again, and to try and understand better how the attack could have occurred.

He had heard of Rasquin, as a Bonapartist camp-follower who moved among the pedlars and backstreet dealers of Paris. But, when he went into Ricord's tavern that Friday evening, it was the first time that he had met him; if he had not known of Rasquin's connections, he would have found the man slightly ridiculous; as it was, he was prepared to ignore the posturing so long as they entered into a real negotiation.

The inn-keeper directed them to the private room. Ricord had cleared away all traces of the deadly meeting between Blake and the actress. The floor was clean, the furniture intact. When he came in with wine for the two men, his keys clanking at his hip, he set the drink down on the table. Then, muttering about needing to fetch something, he opened the door at the back, went into the store-room and came out with half a dozen bottles in his hands. Rougemont could not tell whether Ricord recognised him from his fateful previous visit; the inn-keeper ignored him, and said no more than a few words of greeting to Rasquin. He went about his business as though nothing untoward had taken place in his tavern, no life extinguished there, only forty-eight hours before.

Rougemont produced the pendant, and answered all the questions which Rasquin asked as he examined the

134

object. But the younger man found himself trying to imagine the scene when Blake had been here with Suzanne Pâquerette, his attention drawn to every aspect of the room. And then, to his relief, he heard Rasquin offer to buy the pendant; they agreed a price which satisfied both of them; and it was settled that the exchange should take place at seven on Sunday evening. There was a brief hand-shake, and Rougemont left the tavern, vowing never to return.

By Saturday morning, that vow had grown into a decision to leave Paris altogether. Franklin Blake's wife had left for England the day before; her correct manner and careful expression of gratitude for his hospitality could scarcely conceal her disappointment at Rougemont's failure to support her husband when he was arrested; she made it clear that, though she intended to return to Paris soon, she would not impose upon him again. He was glad of it, glad that he would not have to maintain the pretence of being the host of Rue Marbeuf. Leaving that house meant running the risk of a new hand-to-mouth existence, but he shuddered at the thought of staying there any longer.

There was Ledouin, of course. He would soon be back in the city, looking for him. As he had shown in the past, Ledouin was a man who spared no effort to track others down. And Ledouin knew about all aspects of Rougemont's relationship with Blake, past and present, and could well have seen him put the pendant in his pocket when he visited on the morning after the murder.

He would write Ledouin a letter, which Guillaume could hand over when the investigation agent made his inevitable next visit. He sat down in his drawing-room and put pen to paper. He was surprised by a sudden wish to confess, to acknowledge the regrets that he now felt for bringing Blake to Paris under false pretences, and for guiding him towards the encounter with Suzanne Pâquerette which had such a tragic outcome. Memories of the private room at the *Auberge des Dunes* rushed back into his mind. Far from confirming his belief that Blake had done the killing, they threw him into an abyss of doubt, and this too he set down in his letter to Ledouin. He ended with an assurance that he would stay away from Paris and play no more part in the handling of Blake's case, by the police or by Ledouin himself; and with a plea to the investigation agent not to pursue him.

By Sunday evening, he had packed the clothes and other possessions he needed in a travelling-case, and instructed Guillaume to have it ready for him on his return from his meeting with Rasquin's associate. He gave the butler the letter, sealed and addressed to Ledouin, to be passed to the agent in person. Pulling on a coat against the evening cold, he went out, to walk to the Jardin Marbeuf.

It was scarcely an hour later when the letter was placed in the hands of the addressee. Guillaume could tell Ledouin only that Rougemont had expected to return, collect his case, and leave again that evening, but the young Frenchman had not disclosed where he was going in the interim. Ledouin decided to wait in the drawing-room. The hours went by; the agent was sustained by coffee and cold food brought to him by the butler; he read and re-read the letter until it was word-perfect in his mind; finally, he fell asleep in his chair. Guillaume woke him at the first light of day, to confirm that Rougemont had not returned. Asking to be given word if Rougemont re-appeared in the Rue Marbeuf, Ledouin made for the hotel where he had arrived the night before. Something had gone wrong. He needed to discover what had become of the young Frenchman.

Chapter Eight
Monday 20 September 1852 – Paris

There were two surprises for Boizillac when he reported to the Prefecture of Police that morning.

The first was Delourcq. The older man was slouched by the main entrance, looking more like a convict than a police agent, but grinning broadly.

"Good to see you again!" said Boizillac. "How's the leg?"

"I shan't be dancing in any *bal de barrière* for a few more weeks," he joked. "But I'm back on my feet." He walked a few steps, hobbling slightly. "You didn't run Cotte down?"

The other man shook his head. "I went over the ground thoroughly, and even spoke to old Taillefer. No trace. My luck seemed to disappear when you did."

"Maybe it's returned with me as well, captain." There was a twinkle in his eye. He had news for Boizillac which was the second surprise. "They pulled a body out of the canal this morning. It's in the morgue. I got word while I was waiting for you."

"You think it might be Cotte? But there wouldn't be much left of him if he's been in the canal for the last ten days."

"Depends how hungry the eels were."

"You're right, Delourcq, we should take a look at this body."

The morgue was in the Marché Neuf, on the Ile de la Cité. It took Boizillac and Delourcq less than fifteen minutes to walk there. Even before they entered the building, they caught the unmistakable smell of putrefaction that hung around it. They were not the only visitors. As usual, ordinary Parisians had entered to look through the internal windows that gave on to the mortuary rooms, where the bodies were displayed on slabs. With some, their worried faces showed that they had come to see whether any of the corpses belonged to family members who had gone missing; but most of the onlookers had no personal interest, and were drawn by simple curiosity.

The two men spoke to the morgue-keeper and gained admission to the mortuary area. The keeper took them past three bodies - an old man, a woman, and a young boy - to the corpse that had been in the canal. The man's clothes were hanging on a stand next to the slab, still dripping water; his body was swathed in a sheet, leaving only his head visible.

"Not Jacques Cotte," Delourcq said at once. "This fellow can't have been in the canal for more than twelve hours."

Boizillac was silent for a few moments, looking closely at the face: bleached of colour, and swollen by the water, it was still recognisable. "No, it's not Jacques Cotte. But I know this man. His name is Louis Rougemont, and I saw him in his house last Thursday." He turned to the morgue-keeper. "Has anyone else identified him?"

"No, sir" came the reply. "I looked through all his pockets. Empty."

Boizillac stood with his back to the internal window and moved the covering sheet. "No wounds?"

"No, sir. Simple case of drowning."

As he put the sheet down again, Boizillac paused. "Look at his neck, Delourcq."

The other man did so. "It's scratched and bruised." He looked at the keeper. "Maybe not so simple, after all."

There was a register by the door into the mortuary room. Boizillac went over and opened the heavy ledger. Pointing to the section for that day, he instructed the keeper to add Rougemont's name alongside the entry for "corpse retrieved from Canal Saint-Martin", with details of his address and the fact that it was Boizillac who had made the identification. Then the two men left.

Delourcq had bided his time. Now he looked inquiringly at Boizillac, who explained his visit to the *Auberge des Dunes*, the arrest of Franklin Blake for murdering Suzanne Pâquerette, and his own encounter with Louis Rougemont that same evening. "We'll go to Rue Marbeuf now," he said, hailing a cab.

"And it was Alfred Graize who made the arrest?" Delourcq asked, as they jolted along the streets. "I've heard a few things about him. None of them pleasant."

"He warned me off interfering at the tavern. It's his patch, so I can't object."

"And Rougemont? He was found on Graize's patch." He paused. "Aren't you interfering now?"

"Graize might say so. But I would rather say that I'm helping his investigation, even if he doesn't know yet. It was odd that Rougemont kept quiet about being Blake's friend when the Englishman was arrested. It's even odder that he's been killed now. His death may have nothing to do with what happened last week in the *Auberge des Dunes*, but someone needs to look into it. That's what I intend to do."

"That's good enough for me, captain. Graize may give us the rough edge of his tongue, but that's a flea-bite compared with the knock my leg took!"

When they arrived at the house in the Rue Marbeuf, the door was opened by Guillaume. "I am afraid that the house is empty," he said straightaway. "Monsieur Rougemont is not here."

"I need to speak to you," Boizillac said. "This is my colleague, Daniel Delourcq." The two men stepped inside, and stood in the hallway. The door was closed; the butler waited, with a troubled look on his face. "When did you last see Louis Rougemont?"

"Yesterday evening. He went out at seven o'clock. He said that he would be back after an hour or so - but he has not returned."

"We've just come from the morgue, where we saw the dead body of Louis Rougemont. He was found drowned in the Canal Saint-Martin this morning."

Guillaume crossed himself, and looked bewildered. "Dead? Drowned?" He lapsed into silence.

"When he went out last night, did he say where he was going?"

"No." He was collecting his thoughts. "But he had a case of clothes ready for when he came back."

"Ready for what?"

"To leave Paris."

"Why did he want to leave?"

Guillaume shook his head. "I'm not sure. But I think that he was troubled by the arrest of his English friend.

Once his friend's wife went back to London, on Friday, he made up his mind to leave."

Delourcq had been taking in the grandeur of the house, displayed in the broad staircase ahead of them which rose to the first floor. Now he asked a question: "What do you think will become of you?"

"Me?"

"Yes, now that the master of the house is dead."

Guillaume paused. "Ah. The truth is that Monsieur Rougemont was not really the master."

Boizillac intervened. "What do you mean?"

"It was the patron of Monsieur Rougemont who arranged to rent this house earlier this year, and who engaged my services on his behalf."

Boizillac and Delourcq exchanged a glance. "Patron?" the younger man asked. "Who is this patron? Does he also live here?"

"It's an unusual arrangement, which was not to be acknowledged. But, now that Monsieur Rougemont is dead --" He shook his head. "I never learnt his real name. He introduced himself to me as Monsieur L, and that was the name which Monsieur Rougemont used when he talked to me about him. Monsieur L has never stayed here, but over the last three months he has visited this house every week or two, and he always spent many hours talking to Monsieur Rougemont."

"Talking?"

"I believe that he was giving Monsieur Rougemont instructions, about how to run this house, and how to act as a host to his English visitors."

Delourcq grunted. "Never heard of anything like it."

Boizillac turned to the butler. "And when was this patron last here?"

"Last night. He arrived after Monsieur Rougemont had gone out. He waited for him to return, but in vain."

"And I suppose you don't know how to find this patron?"

Guillaume shook his head. "I don't know where he stays in Paris. But --" He paused. "I expect that he will come back to this house, today or tomorrow, to see whether Monsieur Rougemont has finally returned."

"Very well," said Boizillac. "When he does, you must tell him that I want to speak to him as soon as possible. You know who I am - Captain Lucien de Boizillac, of the Sûreté. Tell him to send a message to me at the Prefecture of Police, with a time and place where I can meet him. Will you do that?"

"Of course," Guillaume replied. "I am sorry to hear that Monsieur Rougemont is dead. He was - well, not the most likeable of men, but he was only half-way through life."

"How old are you?" Delourcq asked.

Guillaume paused and looked his questioner up and down. Beyond the dishevelled mass of greying hair and the coat and trousers that looked as though they had been left out in the rain for months, he recognised someone who had retained a fellow feeling, despite a lifetime of hardship. "Fifty *monsieur*."

"About my age," Delourcq volunteered. "My back aches in the morning when I turn out of bed, my legs ache in the evening when I get home again, and my head aches most of the time from the noise of this wretched city. But I give thanks for being alive, despite all the pains that fifty years have brought - and for not being thrown into a canal to drown."

"Enough philosophy," Boizillac said. "We must move on." Guillaume watched them hail a cab, then retreated into the house, to wait.

* * *

Ledouin planned to go back to the Rue Marbeuf later in the day. But he spent much of the morning in his hotel, reading the letter that Rougemont had left for him, and deciding on his own next steps. He was unsure whether he would prolong his stay in Paris but, at all events, he felt that he should waste no time in letting his client know of Rougemont's disappearance. He wrote to "Mr John Yorkshire" at the finance-house in London and took his letter to the General Post Office in the Rue

Jean-Jacques Rousseau, to make sure that it left for England with the morning departure.

He wanted to speak to Ricord, the inn-keeper, again. What Rougemont had written about his last meeting there settled in Ledouin's mind alongside the scepticism which the investigation agent already felt about Ricord, and his dismissive attitude to Ledouin's questions the day after the murder. He would make another attempt to get information out of the man; if that failed, this time he would let Ricord know what he thought of him.

It was gone eleven o'clock when Ledouin reached the *Auberge des Dunes*; the place was open for business, and there were already drinkers at the tables inside. But there was no sign of the inn-keeper. The drinks were being served by a lumbering young man with the build of a farm-labourer. When Ledouin sat down, the over-sized waiter came up and loomed over him like a dark cloud.

"I would like to talk to Monsieur Ricord."

The younger man failed to understand. "What do you want to drink?"

"I'm not here to drink," Ledouin explained, slowly. "But I do want to talk to the inn-keeper, Monsieur Ricord."

"Ricord?" The waiter looked over his bulging shoulder, towards the bar. "He's not here."

"Has he gone somewhere?"

The younger man shuffled his feet. "You'd have to ask him that."

Ledouin was torn between amusement and irritation. "I can't do that if he isn't here. Do you know where Monsieur Ricord is?" His voice had become louder.

The waiter was struggling to come up with a reply when the door to the private room opened and Ricord appeared. "Leave Émile alone." He beckoned to Ledouin, waited as he crossed to the room, then pulled him in and shut the door firmly.

The table was in the centre, as usual. But behind it, leaning back on a chair that was dwarfed by his form, sat Alfred Graize. Ricord, who went to stand at the left-hand side of the policeman, said in a grudging manner: "This is Olivier Ledouin."

Graize gestured to Ledouin to sit down opposite him. "Why are you here?" he barked.

Ledouin, no stranger to the policeman's manner, took his time before replying. Resisting the temptation to ask the same question, he said: "I went to the house of Monsieur Louis Rougemont yesterday, hoping to speak to him. He wasn't there. But he left me a letter, in which he said that he came hcre last Friday, for a business transaction. I wish to find Monsieur Rougemont again, and I thought that Monsieur Ricord might know something that would help me."

Ricord shot a nervous glance in the direction of Graize, whose attention was fixed solely on the investigation agent. "If you want to find Rougemont, go to the morgue. His dead body was identified there earlier today."

The words were spoken with a coldness that verged on contempt. Ledouin hid his own reaction. After his all-night wait in the house in the Rue Marbeuf, he had feared the worst for the young Frenchman; Graize's news, though chilling, merely confirmed that his fears had been justified. "He was killed?"

"He was fished out of the canal this morning. He drowned. What happened before that is impossible to say." He fixed Ledouin with his gaze. "Why do you think he was killed? What do you know about his death?"

Ledouin raised his hands in protest. "Nothing at all, I assure you. But when a young man leaves his house fit and well one evening, and is found dead in a canal the next morning, it suggests that there may have been foul play."

Graize ignored the suggestion. "Do you have the letter he wrote to you?"

"Not with me. It is in my hotel room."

"What did he say about his visit here?"

Ledouin was aware that Ricord was listening to him no less closely than Graize. "He said that he came here last Friday to discuss a transaction with another person --"

"What transaction? Who was this other person?"

It was the narrowing of the inn-keeper's eyes that decided Ledouin: this was not the moment to disclose everything that Rougemont had put in his letter. "He had a piece of jewellery, made of precious stones, to sell. But who the interested party was, I cannot say."

Graize turned to Ricord, who backed off slightly. "Do you remember Rougemont coming here on Friday?"

"Now that Ledouin mentions it, yes."

"Do you know who met him?"

Ricord shrugged his shoulders. "He was a shabby-looking character, with a face-full of whiskers." He went on quickly. "Not a beard like yours, but a wispy sort of moustache and a streak of hair on his chin." He grinned sourly. "No a leader of men."

"Did you hear their conversation?"

The question seemed to spark a flash of anger in Ricord's face. "Why would I want to eavesdrop on those two? Anyway, they met in this room, in private."

"And when they left, did they look as if they had quarrelled?"

"They shook hands, like old friends." The sour grin reappeared on Ricord's face. "But what does that mean? Judas kissed Jesus."

Graize turned back to Ledouin. "It may be that Rougemont died naturally, or by his own hand. But I am looking into the circumstances of his death, which is why I was questioning Ricord about anything that he might have seen or heard last night. I shall consider the information that you have provided about Rougemont's meeting on Friday. Even if Ricord did not recognise the man that he met, others may have done so. The letter that Rougemont left for you may be helpful to me, and I would ask you to pass it to me at the earliest opportunity. Which hotel are you staying in? How long are you in Paris?"

"The Hotel Victoria, in the Rue Chauveau Lagarde. I haven't decided how long to stay."

"Then make sure that you leave the letter at the Prefecture of Police by the end of the day." He nodded peremptorily at Ledouin. "You may leave now. I need to speak further with Ricord."

Ledouin needed no second asking. He had come to the *Auberge des Dunes* to see if he could find out what had happened to Rougemont; the quest had been solved. It would be impossible to get Ricord to say any more than Graize had compelled him to do; but there had been several unspoken signals by Ricord which Ledouin wanted to think through, on his own. He got up and left, keenly aware of the inn-keeper's hostile gaze on him as he went.

The cab ride back to his hotel allowed him to think through the conversation. His instinct for caution had guided him away from revealing all that he knew, but he felt uneasy that he had told Graize and Ricord where he was staying. That was a mistake he could remedy. He settled his bill at the Hotel Victoria, saying that he had decided to return to England that day. In fact, he moved half a mile across the city to a less prominent establishment, the Hotel Beauséjour, in the Rue de Provence: still not sure how long he would stay, he preferred to keep his location, and his intentions, to himself.

He took lunch in a nearby restaurant. Though he had little appetite, he knew from experience that missing a meal left him slower of thought; and he needed to think hard now. He read Rougemont's letter again, and saw in his mind's eye the private room in the tavern and the inn-keeper's unfriendly face. It was almost as though there was a seam of evil under the place, which had seen Suzanne Pâquerette put to death, and Rougemont himself embroiled in a transaction which proved fatal. Could Graize be expected to dig deep enough get to the bottom of it?

Graize. Would he visit Rougemont's house? Ledouin decided that he needed to go back there himself as soon as possible. Rougemont might have left other papers that were better not discovered by the police; and Ledouin needed to speak again to the staff at the house.

It was mid-afternoon when he reached the Rue Marbeuf. After waiting long enough to check that there were no other visitors, he went up to the house and knocked at the door.

"Ah, it is you, *monsieur*" said Guillaume as he opened it. "Come in."

Ledouin stepped inside. "I regret to say that, since I left here this morning, I have learnt that Louis Rougemont has met his death." He was concerned in case the servant was shocked by the news. But it was Ledouin who was surprised by Guillaume's response.

"I know," he said simply. "I am sorry for it."

"You know? How? Have the police been here?"

"They have, *monsieur*, this morning."

"Inspector Graize?"

Guillaume shook his head. "I don't know that name. No, it was Captain Boizillac, who came here last week, and another man called Delourcq."

"And they told you about Rougemont's death?" He nodded. "What else happened?"

Guillaume coughed nervously. "They asked about this house, *monsieur*. I explained that you had rented it for Monsieur Rougemont."

"Did you?" Ledouin said, unguardedly. "And what else did you tell them about me?"

"Only that I knew you simply as Monsieur L, but I had no idea where you stayed. I hope that I did the right thing, *monsieur*."

"If that was all you said, Guillaume, there's nothing to worry about."

Guillaume looked relieved, then added: "The captain asked that, if I saw you again, I should tell you that he would like to speak to you himself, as soon as possible. And that you should send a message to the Prefecture of Police, to say when and where you could meet him." He paused. "I have been thinking about poor Monsieur Rougemont all day. I can't imagine what happened to him - but I got the impression that Captain Boizillac would dig away until he found out the truth."

Ledouin was struck by the way in which Guillaume's words echoed his own thoughts about Graize, but to contrasting effect. He told Guillaume that he needed half an hour to look through any papers or possessions that Rougemont had left in the house, and asked that, if any more police came to the door, the steward should delay them while Ledouin made a hidden departure from the house. His search was not interrupted, but failed to produce anything useful. Assuring the steward that he would be in touch with him again soon, he made his way back to his hotel.

He had to choose between several possible courses of action. He could cut and run, saying no more to the police, washing his hands of the complications of the last week, and telling his client that there were no more loose ends, now that Rougemont was dead. That would be simplest. But it might be unwise to slight Graize by ignoring his request to see Rougemont's letter: who knew whether some future investigation might bring him back to Paris, and to cross the policeman's path again?

He could get the letter to Graize and leave straightaway. That seemed the most sensible option, which would keep him on the right side of the police. He might be well-advised to take no further interest in the unravelling of what had happened to the young Frenchman who had been playing the part for which the agent had paid him. But Ledouin had not been indifferent to Rougemont in life, and the sympathy he had felt for him, and his conscience, made him keen to see his death properly investigated and explained. He had a strong sense that Graize might not be the right man to do so.

There was a third possibility. He had seen how Boizillac had battened on to Rougemont after the killing in the *Auberge des Dunes*; and how he had returned to the Rue Marbeuf that morning after identifying Rougemont's body. Guillaume was a good judge of character: perhaps this other policeman would be more committed to getting at the truth; perhaps Ledouin should respond to Boizillac's approach.

Ledouin decided - to delay a decision. The Hotel Beauséjour could provide its guests with modest fare: he sat down to a supper of herb-cooked chicken, with a carafe of robust red wine, and let his digestive system strengthen his powers of thought. He would spend another night in Paris; in the morning, he would make his choice between the possibilities.

Chapter Nine
Tuesday 21 September 1852 - Paris - Rue de Nevers

Antoine Denonvilliers had been an attorney in Paris for almost as many years as Matthew Bruff had been in practice in London. He admired the English in general, as a people who combined a firm legal system with a vigorous promotion of industry and commerce, and who had seen no need to turn their state on its head several times as they progressed to the middle of the century. And he admired Mr Bruff in particular, as the embodiment of English virtues - common sense and cunning, courtesy and confidence. Over the years, they had dealt with each other a number of times, on behalf of clients who were citizens of one country and had become enmeshed in the laws of the other. Their co-operation had always been successful, and left the two men with a deep mutual respect.

Denonvilliers understood that there was a particular bond between Bruff and the young woman who accompanied him that morning to the chambers in Rue de Nevers, and that the English lawyer held her views in high regard. The letter from Mr Bruff which reached him the day before had spoken of her intelligence and self-possession, and advised Denonvilliers, whose services she wished to retain, to explain matters to her with all candour. He had prepared for this interview accordingly.

The French attorney spoke English well, but, whether using his own language or that of his neighbours across the Channel, invariably fell back on the Latin phrases that he had learnt decades before at university. As he guided his visitors towards chairs in his office where they could sit for their discussion, he greeted them warmly. "Mrs Blake, I hope that I can assist you. Mr Bruff, I am pleased to see you again *in propria persona*."

"And I you, Maître Denonvilliers." The two men shook hands. The young woman sat down quickly, and looked to Bruff: it was clear that she wanted to proceed to business without delay.

"May I ask if you have seen my husband, Maître Denonvilliers?" Her question was spoken in a firm voice, but with an urgency that hinted at the emotion behind it.

"That has not been possible so far, Mrs Blake."

"My letter will have reached Maître Denonvilliers only late yesterday, Rachel," Bruff explained.

"Of course, forgive me."

"But I intend to see Mr Blake *summa celeritate*."

Bruff saw the puzzlement on the young woman's face. "With all possible speed."

"Today?"

The French attorney nodded. "This afternoon. In the meantime, I am indebted to Mr Bruff for the very extensive information about the case which he sent me. And I have also had the opportunity to speak this morning to Maître Favrier, the *juge d'instruction* who is in charge of this case."

"Have you indeed? That is excellent." Bruff turned to his female companion. "You remember that I explained that here in France the *juge d'instruction* investigates the circumstances surrounding a crime --"

"-- and decides whether the accused person should stand trial. Yes, I do remember."

Bruff smiled briefly at her, then turned back to Denonvilliers. "And what did you discover from Maître Favrier? Presumably he has more to do to carry his inquiries through."

The Frenchman paused for a moment, and his face took on a serious look. "Maître Favrier has already completed his investigation and has committed the case to trial." He shook his head. "*Tempus fugit.*"

Both Bruff and Rachel were taken aback by the news. The young woman spoke first. "Mr Bruff told me that the process of investigation could take weeks. How can the case of my husband have been resolved in a matter of days?"

"Come now, Maître," Bruff added. "You must tell us what you know - and what you infer."

"Well then, I shall be open with you." He looked towards the Englishman as he spoke. "Favrier had before him a compelling dossier of evidence relating to the case, showing *primo* that Mr Blake knew Mademoiselle Pâquerette from his stay in Paris some five years ago; *secundo* that Mr Blake went to the tavern last Wednesday in response to a summons from Mademoiselle Pâquerette, who was threatening to make their earlier liaison public." His gaze moved towards the young woman seated next to Bruff; her expression was fixed. "The dossier set out *tertio* that Mr Blake and Mademoiselle Pâquerette were alone in a private room at the tavern, to which no-one else could gain admittance; and *quartum et ultimum*, that, when a disturbance was heard in the room after the two people had been in it for an hour or more, and the door was forced open, Mademoiselle Pâquerette was discovered beaten to death, and Mr Blake lay slumped on top of her, in a state of advanced intoxication."

The last dozen words shattered Rachel's composure; sobbing, she put her hand to her mouth, and shut her eyes as if to banish the image which the French lawyer had conjured up.

Bruff leaned across and put his arm around her shoulders. "You need not hear all of our discussion, Rachel."

But the young woman had recovered. Her eyes glittered fiercely. "Forgive a moment's weakness,

Maître Denonvilliers." Gently, but firmly, she pushed Bruff's arm away. "I do need to hear everything. Pray continue."

"The dossier was prepared, I presume, by the police officer who arrested Franklin Blake?" Bruff asked.

"Yes, by Inspector Graize. Favrier told me that Graize is respected, if not feared, for his rigour and integrity. His words to me were: 'If Graize has presented this evidence, a trial is unavoidable.'"

"But surely Monsieur Favrier must speak to my husband as well, before deciding on whether he should face trial."

"He did so yesterday - before I had received Mr Bruff's letter."

"Yesterday? And did Monsieur Favrier tell you anything of that interview?"

Denonvilliers paused for a moment. "He was impressed by the firmness of your husband's denial that he had caused any harm to Mademoiselle Pâquerette, but he was no less struck by Mr Blake's inability to explain his state of intoxication, or to recall what had happened during the hour that he spent in the room with her. In short, Favrier told me that the lack of any other explanation for the death of Mademoiselle Pâquerette, and the force of the evidence presented by Inspector Graize, made it necessary for him to commit Mr Blake to trial."

"Most unfortunate," Bruff said, shaking his head. "But commitment to trial does not mean a presumption of guilt?"

"No, indeed," the French lawyer responded. "It means that the evidence that has been presented, or that may still be found, will be tested before a judge in court."

"Mr Bruff tells me that you have many years of experience of arguing before the courts of Paris. Will you defend my husband in this trial, Maître Denonvilliers? He may have acted foolishly in his dealings with that unfortunate woman, but he is innocent of her murder, even if he is accused of it."

"*Accusare facilius est quam defendere.*" He offered his own translation. "It is easier to accuse than to defend. I stood ready to defend your husband once I received the letter from Mr Bruff. I am even more resolved to do so now that I have had this conversation with Mr Bruff and yourself."

There were details to be discussed, and Denonvilliers talked with his English visitors for another half-hour. But for the first time in a week, Rachel felt hope enter her mind, a sense that she, and Messrs Bruff and Denonvilliers, had started work on a plan that could lift Franklin out of the mire into which he had fallen.

***

Tuesday 21 September - Paris - Chien Fou

Boizillac sat in the bar with a plate of bread and meat in front of him. He and Delourcq had spent the morning on separate tasks. The older man had gone to renew his acquaintance with the idlers and chancers who lived on the edge of the criminal underworld, to see what he could learn from them about Rougemont and any contacts he had made during the last week. Boizillac had forced himself to enter the offices of the Prefecture of Police, ostensibly to complete the written reports on his activities which he had neglected for some weeks. His real motive, though, was his hope that he would hear from Rougemont's patron.

He was not disappointed. Towards the end of the morning, a messenger left not one, but two letters at the Prefecture, one addressed to himself, the other to Alfred Graize, but both written in the same hand. Boizillac had told the front desk that he was awaiting a message, and the officer on duty alerted him without delay. Boizillac saw the matching letter to Graize and, since the other man was not in the building, was momentarily tempted to take both. He resisted the idea, and left with his own letter to seek the privacy of the *Chien Fou*. He had read it once, and now considered it a second time.

"Paris, 21 September 1852
Dear Captain Boizillac
Guillaume passed on to me your invitation to contact you. I do so with this letter. I must for now decline your proposal of a meeting, but I trust that the information which I provide herewith will serve your purposes equally well.

162

*Louis Rougemont was not a man of independent wealth.
I supplied him with the means to establish and maintain
his household in the Rue Marbeuf. Five years ago he
associated for some months with Franklin Blake during
the time that Mr Blake spent in Paris. There had been
no contact between the two men after Mr Blake's
departure from the city, until I persuaded M.
Rougemont to approach Mr Blake once again earlier
this year, and to invite him to return to Paris.*

*You will ask why I did so. I can say only that I was in
turn acting on behalf of a client - an English client -
who is antipathetic to Mr Blake and saw, in Mr Blake's
return to a city where he had committed youthful
indiscretions, the opportunity to expose him to scandal
and disgrace.*

*That Mr Blake now sits in prison accused of murder
must seem, at first glance, to be the perfect realisation
of this opportunity. I urge you, however, to believe my
assurance that the fatal outcome of that reunion
between Mr Blake and Mademoiselle Pâquerette was
never intended, by my client or by myself. It is a source
of deep regret to me, as it was also to M. Rougemont.
I know this, because on Sunday, two days ago, shortly
before he left the house in Rue Marbeuf to go to his
death, M. Rougemont penned a letter to me in which he
wrote of his remorse over the part that he had played in
bringing Mr Blake back to Paris and guiding him
towards his disgrace.*

*None of this may assist you very far in your
investigations. But other details in that letter (which I*

163

shall retain for the present) may prove salient. You know that M. Rougemont was in the Auberge des Dunes *last Wednesday, when the fateful encounter took place. You may not know that he returned to the tavern last Friday, to discuss a transaction involving the sale of a precious stone that he had received from Franklin Blake (I shall not dwell on the background, save to assure you that I believe that Mr Blake passed it to M. Rougemont in good faith, and as a sign of friendship).*

Two details stand out.

First, on Friday, M. Rougemont was in the private room where Mademoiselle Pâquerette was earlier done to death. He noticed that the landlord carried keys to open the outer door, to the main tavern area, and the inner door, to the store-room - but so did the serving-man, Émile, who came and unlocked the inner door while the landlord stood talking to other customers. When the landlord was questioned on Wednesday evening, he said that he carried the only key to the store-room.

Second, he wrote that he had agreed to complete the transaction, and hand over the stone in return for money, later on Sunday. His letter gave no name for the purchaser, and no place for the exchange, but you may agree that this transaction may be closely linked with his disappearance and death.

Forgive me if I am unable to give you all the information which you may well wish to obtain. I cannot disclose the name of my client, nor the reason for his antipathy towards Mr Blake, and I prefer to withhold from you my own name. I hope, nonetheless, that you will accept my goodwill in setting out such details as I have now done, with as much candour as I can offer. Guillaume's belief in your ability to expose the reason for M. Rougemont's death has swayed me to be as forthcoming in this letter as I have felt possible. I have also written to Inspector Graize but, I confess, not at such length as to you.

With respect
L"

He was looking intently at the letter when Delourcq slumped down on a chair next to him. "Good news?" the older man asked.

"It's from Monsieur L, as Guillaume calls him. It was left at the Prefecture this morning. He's turned down my suggestion of a meeting, but there's plenty of food for thought in his letter."

"Talking of food, are you going to eat that?" Boizillac pushed the plate to Delourcq, who quickly cleared it. "So, what does he say?"

"Louis Rougemont went to sell a precious stone to a third party on the night he was killed. Before that, last Friday, he went back to the *Auberge des Dunes* to discuss the transaction, and realised that the landlord had been lying when he told Alfred Graize there was only one key to open the door between the private room and the back-store, because Rougemont saw Émile use a second key."

165

Delourcq chewed thoughtfully for a few seconds. "I've got something to tell you about Ricord, the landlord, and the man Émile, after my conversations this morning. But what is this precious stone? Anything to do with the Englishman and the dead woman?"

"Monsieur L says only that Blake passed the stone to Rougemont. There's more to be found out about it, I'm sure. But what stands out is the way so much leads back to the *Auberge des Dunes*. Suzanne Pâquerette was murdered there; Rougemont met the prospective purchaser of this stone there; and the stretch of the canal where his body was found is only a minute or two away from the tavern, isn't it?"

Delourcq wiped his mouth with the back of his hand. "Well, here's what I've learnt this morning. Ricord, the landlord, has run the place for ten years or more. By all accounts, his wine is good and his food wholesome, even if the man himself is as acid as vinegar. The tavern has a good reputation and a lot of regular customers.

"But that wasn't always the case. After old Pear-Face was kicked out - the old Orleanist king, I mean - the tavern fell on hard times and came near to closing. Ricord had always made a great show of his support for the Orleanists, and when they flew the coop, his old clientèle went into hiding.

"It took the rise of Badinguet - the Prince-President, I should say - to save the tavern from extinction. For the last three years, the *Auberge des Dunes* has gone from strength to strength. Ricord has turned his coat, and his pockets have never been fuller."

"Turned his coat?"

"Thrown in his lot with the Bonapartists. At least once a week, that private room is used by one or other of the Prince-President's hangers-on, to do whatever they do. Plan ways to drive the poor out of Paris, no doubt."

Boizillac ignored the provocation: he was used to Delourcq's contempt for government, especially the present one, and knew that it was no more than a reflex action in speaking. "You can't hold it against Ricord if he's found a way to keep his tavern going."

Delourcq had acquired a glass of wine. "Well, I wouldn't drink there." He swallowed a mouthful, and grunted in appreciation. "Some of the company would spoil the taste of the drink. Have you met any of these johnny-come-lately types who are riding on Badinguet's coat-tails?" Boizillac shook his head. "None of them had more than two sous to rub together until a couple of years ago, and now they strut around like cocks on dung-heaps.   There's one in particular - Charles Rasquin. He looks like a scarecrow that's been dressed in cast-off clothes, and he's full of hints and whispers about the connections he has with our new rulers. I've seen him around before, but I found out this morning that he's a regular at Ricord's place." He drained his glass. "As a matter of fact, one of my informants seemed to think he saw Rasquin there last Friday, slinking in and out of a meeting in that private room."

"Last Friday?" Boizillac repeated. "So, it could have been this Rasquin who met Rougemont to discuss this stone. Your informant didn't see who else was in the room?" Delourcq shook his head. "Did you learn anything else this morning?"

"Well, like I said before, there's no love lost between Ricord and many of the locals, even if he has managed to pack the tavern with Bonapartist sympathisers. He had a couple of serving staff until earlier this year, but he sacked them with no good reason this summer, and replaced them with this Émile - as strong as an ox, and twice as stupid. Ricord must be saving money on wages, but you don't send Goliath to do the job of a waiter." He lowered his voice. "The word is that Émile used his fists to help the Bonapartists at some of their rallies, and Ricord took him on as a favour to them." Delourcq gave a wry smile. "All in all, captain, the *Auberge des Dunes* is about the last place I'd choose to spend my money."

"I think we'll have to go back there before too long. But I'd like to see this Charles Rasquin and talk to him. Do you know where we can find him?"

Delourcq had not neglected this detail either: their best chance of catching Rasquin off-guard would be the next morning, at the Marché des Innocents. Until then, and with some reluctance, the two men returned to the task of following up rumours about resistance to the new regime. It was an afternoon of visits to run-down houses in shady side-streets: both men were tacitly pleased that none of these harboured anyone worthy of arrest.

Tuesday 21 September 1852 – Paris - Rue de Grenelle 103

Night had fallen on the city. While others sought pleasure in bars or restaurants, Victor de Persigny sat in his office on the top floor of his Ministry building, reading letters, memorandums and reports by the light of the candles that flickered above his desk. He had travelled back from Lyon during the day, leaving the Prince-President to continue on his triumphal tour of the provinces. Now he could read the accounts sent in by his network of informers of the private reactions of the crowds who had lined the roads for the earlier stages of the visits: there was some mockery, yes, but Persigny was pleased to read that the great majority of comments showed enthusiasm for Louis-Napoléon, and for the prospect of a return of the Empire. Even allowing for the inevitable exaggeration of support by informers keen to please, Persigny was reassured that the Bonapartist project was making good progress.

There was a knock at the door. His private secretary looked in and said: "A Monsieur Rasquin is in the outer office."

Persigny signalled that the visitor should be admitted. He had sent word earlier in the day that the man should call on him at eight. He looked at the clock: Rasquin might have the airs of a posing marionette, but he knew the virtue of punctuality.

Top-hat and cane in one hand, leather pouch in the other, Rasquin swept in and bowed deeply. "Monsieur

169

le Ministre, I congratulate you on your safe return to Paris."

Persigny had no time for conversational fripperies. "The pendant, Rasquin?"

The other man's face lit up, and he extended the pouch. "The pendant, Monsieur." He placed it respectfully on the desk and stepped back. "An antique and historic piece.   I am delighted to be the conduit for its transmission to you, and through you, to --" He left the rest unsaid.

Persigny took the object out of the pouch, and stood up to hold it directly under one of the candle-sconces on the wall. He turned it to and fro, and saw the light sparkle on the silver frame and the surface of the red stones.   For a second, he felt the energy that the craftsman of ancient times must have put into shaping the pendant: his hands tingled, as though a real bee had made its trembling way across them.

"It is remarkable, Rasquin." There was another bow. Persigny fitted the pendant back in the pouch, then went to a cabinet in a corner of the room; leaving the pouch inside it, he came back with an envelope which he gave to the other man.   "Here is the remainder of the payment."

"I thank you, Monsieur le Ministre. It is an honour and a privilege to be able to assist you." He drew himself up and, head held back, filled his lungs with the Ministerial atmosphere. "I shall continue to serve you as best I can."

"Thank you." Persigny took his seat again behind his desk and gave his visitor a brief smile, as if to dismiss him. Rasquin tilted his head one more time, and started to stride purposefully towards the door. "Remind me of who sold you the pendant."

He stopped in his tracks. It took him a moment to realise that he was not after all being sent away. Turning to face Persigny, he spoke again: "A young man called Louis Rougemont."

The Minister was looking through his papers. "And your associate met Rougemont on Sunday evening, to purchase the pendant from him."

"Exactly, Monsieur le Ministre."

"You were not there?"

"Why no, Monsieur, I was on my way to see you."

"But you have since spoken to your associate?" Rasquin nodded. "Did he describe his meeting with Rougemont?"

"It went as planned, Monsieur. My associate travelled in a carriage to the Jardin Marbeuf, at seven o'clock. Rougemont joined him in the carriage and they rode through the streets while the pendant was produced on one side and the payment on the other and, after both had been examined satisfactorily, the exchange was made, the carriage returned to the Jardin Marbeuf, and Rougemont stepped down, with one hundred francs in his pocket." He attempted a smile. "A good night's work, Monsieur le Ministre."

Persigny picked up a sheet of paper from his desk and read from it. "Report by Graize, Alfred, inspector of police, Saint-Martin quarter. Monday 20 September 1852. Body recovered this morning from Canal Saint-Martin and displayed at morgue, identified as Rougemont, Louis. Cause of death assumed to be drowning. Clothing of deceased examined at morgue, pockets empty. Investigation to be taken forward. Et cetera." He looked up at Rasquin. "Who is your associate?"

The other man was twisting his moustaches in an agitated fashion. "If Monsieur le Ministre insists on knowing his name -- he is my brother, Eustache Rasquin."

"And did your brother decide to keep the payment as well as the pendant, and ensure that Rougemont could not complain?"

"Eustache? No, a thousand times no, Monsieur."

Persigny looked at him for a few moments. "Very well, Rasquin. I rely on your word that your associate - your brother - paid for the pendant in the way you described. But he did so only hours before Rougemont lost his life in the waters of the canal. If others were to learn about the transaction that took place on Sunday evening, it would be hard to counteract suspicion about your brother's involvement. Let us decide to keep all this a secret between ourselves."

"Most assuredly, Monsieur."

"Good. As I say, I rely on you, Rasquin. And those who rely on me are no less dependent on your resolution." The other man fixed his face in an expression of determination. "That is all. I am sure that we shall benefit from your service again."

Rasquin's march to the door was not interrupted this time. As he made his way out into the darkness of the Rue de Grenelle, Persigny's words still rang in his ears: he, and others behind and above the Minister, relied on him. Rasquin would not let them down.

Chapter Ten

Wednesday 22 September 1852 - Paris - Rue de Grenelle 103

It was the following day. Persigny had left the Ministry late and returned early. As the morning lightened, he admitted another visitor whom he had summoned to his office: Alfred Graize.

Unlike Rasquin, Graize wasted no time on demonstrations of servility, and had no scruples about sitting down in the presence of the Minister. He might not be his equal in terms of status, but he had no doubt about his utility to the regime, as an enforcer of law and order. He kept his silence, waiting for the other man to speak.

"You have heard about the success of the Prince-President's tour of the provinces?" Persigny began. Graize nodded briefly. "All of France is rallying to his cause. But we must be in no doubt. The road to the Empire can still be blocked at the last minute, and this city is where any road-block is most likely to be thrown up." He paused and looked at the policeman.

"Scum gathers where most filth flows," Graize muttered.

"And there is still too much scum in the streets of Paris," Persigny blustered. "We are cleaning it up, but the task is never-ending." He shook his head in regret. "The role of the police is essential. What you have already done has been invaluable. But I asked you here today because of events that have happened in the city over the last week."

"The murder of the actress, and the death of Rougemont." His voice was a low rumble.

"Yes. I have seen your reports. I commend you. You leave no doubts about the culpability of this Englishman for killing the woman."

"He goes on trial soon. He is sure to be found guilty."

"That will be a satisfactory resolution to the case." There was a look of understanding between the two men. "But what of Rougemont?"

"He was a fool, and a greedy one. I now believe that he was robbed and murdered, and his body thrown into the canal. But the chances of finding his killer are negligible."

Persigny stood up and walked to a window. "I have received some relevant information. Last Friday, Rougemont had a meeting at the *Auberge des Dunes*, with a third party. Did you know this?"

"Yes. The landlord, Ricord, has confirmed as much. But he denies any knowledge of who it was that met Rougemont."

"The man was Charles Rasquin," Persigny said. "I am sure you recognise the name. Rasquin has worked for us, for me in particular, for some time now. He may appear to be a man of straw, but he has served me well." Graize remained impassive. "Rasquin agreed to arrange for Rougemont to be paid for the object, a piece of jewellery, which he wanted to sell. Rougemont received the payment from Rasquin's brother on Sunday evening, and went away from that second meeting in good health. Rasquin was acting on my behalf." Persigny came back to the desk. "It was not Rasquin, or his brother, who killed Rougemont. You need to look elsewhere."

"Rasquin?" Graize echoed. "I know him. He hangs about the Saint-Martin quarter like a bad smell."

"You must hold your nose when you meet him. We need him." He sat down. "But, Ricord."

Graize raised his eyebrows. "The keeper of the *Auberge des Dunes*?"

"What do you make of him?"

"He knows his business, and his customers, and he does what the police tell him."

"What you tell him," Persigny clarified. Graize nodded. "Rasquin has used his tavern before. His face must have been familiar to Ricord, but you say that the inn-keeper claimed not to know the man who met Rougemont on Friday. I find that hard to believe."

Graize considered this. "I'll talk to Ricord again. If he did not recognise Rasquin, I need do no more. But if he knew him and told me otherwise, I shall press him hard to explain. And I shall make sure that he keeps the name to himself."

"Will he be called as a witness at the trial of the Englishman?"

"That is possible," Graize muttered.

"Can we be sure of what he might say in the court-room?"

"I'll speak to him about that as well." He paused. "He has no reason to refer to Rougemont, or his death."

"But he could be asked about it."

"I'll make sure he says nothing untoward."

"Your service will not go unrewarded." He pointed to the reports on his desk. "Everywhere, our countrymen are calling for the return of the Empire. It needs strong and loyal servants to bring it about, and to ensure that it prospers." His voice rose as he spoke. "We are on the threshold of a new era. We cannot allow our progress to be held up by scandal-mongering, about the murder of an actress in a tavern, or about the killing of a dealer in precious objects. We cannot allow it!" He brought

177

his fist down on his desk to emphasise the point. Graize kept his own counsel, but his eyes glittered fiercely. "I must not detain you any longer, but I thank you for what you have done, and what you will do."

The policeman stood up. With a brief and sonorous "Your servant", he turned and left the room. He had made no mention of Ledouin, and the letter from him that he had collected at the Prefecture the day before. It would suit no-one to concern the Minister about the involvement of that particular third party; the man's letter contained little more than he had already said in person, and was in any case best followed up in Graize's dealings with Ricord.

Persigny reflected on the contrast between Rasquin, devoted to the Bonapartist cause but malleable and contorted, like a twisted vine; and Graize, solid like an old oak, but true above all to his own interest and advantage. He needed both of them to work for him, but he found it hard to gauge which man served the cause better. He would watch them both carefully.

***

Wednesday 22 September 1852 - Paris - Marché des Innocents

Boizillac and Delourcq stood outside the huge, dilapidated, wooden shed that housed the different markets in the Place du Marché des Innocents. The younger man looked doubtful.

"Trust me, captain, I've been told Rasquin spends most of his mornings parading around the markets, bragging about his connections and trying to fool the market-holders into giving him free samples of their goods."

"This place looks as if it could fall down at any moment. No wonder the Government wants to demolish it."

Delourcq spat on the ground. "And who will carry the cost of rebuilding the halls? It'll be the stall-owners, and their customers, while the Government gets all the glory."

Boizillac smiled. "Better than having the roof fall in. Lead the way, Delourcq."

They went in through the main entrance. Stalls stretched away on either side, selling bread, fruit, vegetables, fish and flowers. Noise filled the air, as prices were shouted out, insults were hurled between traders, barrows creaked over the stones, and water was tipped from buckets to sluice away discards dropped on the ground. As they paused to get their bearings, the two men were jostled by the constant flow of housewives and servants pushing in to choose from the produce on display or hurrying out to carry their purchases home. There was a loud shout: "You look like a couple of fish out of water - come over here and I'll put you on my slab!" It was a woman fishmonger: she stood behind a stall selling *fruits de mer*, and shared her laughter with her neighbours.

"Come on, captain. From the look of her, she might not be joking!"

Boizillac had never visited the market before; it seemed to him now almost like a town within the city, teeming with all ages and types of men and women. None of the faces were known to him, but he noticed that Delourcq was greeted by quite a few of the people who passed by along the central thoroughfare. Even as he returned their greetings, Delourcq was scanning the scene on all sides; and after a couple of minutes he stopped and said to Boizillac: "There he is, over there, by the stall selling bread."

The roof windows dropped pools of light into the shadowed interior. In one of them Boizillac could see a figure who stood out even in the jumble of mankind filling the halls: dressed in a battered black greatcoat, he seemed to be gesticulating at the stall-holder with the crumpled hat he held in his left hand, while his right clutched a cane. As his face turned back and forth, it showed off his prominent moustache and beard, which fluttered like pennants that had been shredded by strong winds. "So that's Rasquin?" Delourcq nodded. "Good." He moved towards him.

"Might make a better impression if I hung back and let you approach him on your own," the older man suggested. It was agreed.

The bread stall was run by a couple, husband and wife, who looked at least as old as Delourcq. The woman, a short dumpy figure wearing a rough-stitched apron that was dusted with flour, was dealing with the customers for the loaves and pastries on sale. The man, taller than his wife by a head but no less heavy, directed all his attention towards Rasquin, listening to him with his mouth slightly agape.

"Oh yes, I assure and affirm to you that the new Emperor will usher in an age of prosperity and wealth. We shall all have money in our pockets, money we can spend on the essentials of life, such as your fine bread, as well as the little luxuries, such as the gâteaux I have seen on your stall from time to time. Why, I was speaking to one of the Emperor's closest associates only yesterday --"

"Charles Rasquin?" Boizillac interrupted.

The addressee turned to see who had spoken his name. Noting Boizillac's frock-coat and boots, Rasquin extended his arms and bowed his head in greeting. "The very same. And you, sir?"

"Lucien de Boizillac." Mention of the aristocratic particle in his name had the expected effect: Rasquin's eyes widened approvingly, and he leaned engagingly towards the other man.

"I am pleased to meet you, Monsieur de Boizillac. May I ask, and inquire, what has prompted you to seek me out here? Are you also a supporter of our new Emperor?"

"The Prince-President?" Boizillac corrected him. "I work for his Government."

"Indeed? In what capacity?"

"As an officer in the Sûreté."

It was as if someone had poured a bucket of cold water over Rasquin. His unctuous manner disappeared as he pulled himself backwards, muttered: "Forgive me, I cannot stay any longer", and swung round to hasten away into the crowd.

If Boizillac was surprised by this sudden departure, Delourcq was not. Watching the scene from a short distance, the older man allowed Rasquin to take twenty paces before forcing his way to his side and grabbing hold of his wrist. "Daniel Delourcq, of the Sûreté." He felt the other man shake at the contact.

"Release me. I must keep an appointment."

"This is your appointment," Delourcq countered, nodding towards Boizillac who had now caught up with them. He let go of the other man.

Rasquin made a show of pulling his coat straight: the tucks and creases were momentarily smoothed, then re-formed. "You have no right to detain me. I have the confidence of the Emperor's closest associates."

"We do not intend to detain you, Monsieur Rasquin, or at least not for any longer than we need to ask you one or two questions."

Caught between Boizillac, with his air of well-bred assurance, and Delourcq, with his hint of *sans-culottes* disdain, Rasquin saw no escape. Leaning on his cane, he looked into the middle distance and said: "If you insist. But I have no idea or inkling of why you would wish to question me."

"You know the *Auberge des Dunes*?" Boizillac asked. The other man was immobile, though his eyes narrowed at the question. "Monsieur Rasquin?"

"The *Auberge des Dunes*? I cannot deny or refute that I have visited the tavern on occasions." He spoke to the air, not to his interrogator. "The landlord is a staunch supporter of the Emperor, and it is only natural that I and other followers of the cause come together there from time to time."

"Jean-Marie Ricord. You know him well?"

"Oh, as to that, I know him no better than a well-dressed man knows his tailor." Instinctively, Rasquin brushed one hand over his coat.

"And when were you last there?"

The reply was delayed. "There? At Ricord's tavern?"

"Yes. When was your last visit?"

"I speak for the cause in so many places. It is not easy to be precise and exact."

"Last Friday?" Rasquin ran his finger around his collar. "Were you at the *Auberge des Dunes* last Friday?"

"It -- it is possible. But I recall nothing of import from last Friday." There was sweat on his brow.

"Not even a meeting with one Louis Rougemont?"

His face flushed red. "It is stifling in here. I must have some air." He made a movement as if to leave, but Delourcq blocked him.

"We need only another minute or two of your time, Monsieur Rasquin. It is a simple question. Did you meet Louis Rougemont at the *Auberge des Dunes* on Friday?"

Rasquin's eyes were bulging and he seemed to be panting. "I -- I cannot tell you. You must ask Ricord. He knows who comes and goes to his tavern. For myself, I can say nothing more." He wiped his brow and, recovering his composure, stood up straight. "Monsieur de Boizillac, I have broken no laws, and I act with the knowledge and support of the Emperor's most trusted associates. I feel no constraint or obligation to submit any longer to your questions, and I wish you good day."

At a sign from the younger man, Delourcq stood aside. They watched as Rasquin scuttled away, to leave the market. "What a bag of wind!" Delourcq spat out.

"And none too happy about our questions."

"What about this stuff about the Emperor's associates? If he does have any connections, it could make life difficult."

184

Boizillac's voice took on a determined edge. "We'll cross that bridge when we come to it. For the moment, I propose that we take up his suggestion of talking to Ricord, at the *Auberge des Dunes*."

"As you wish, captain, though I don't suppose he'll be any keener to answer your questions than Rasquin."

"Let's find out." The two men threaded their way out of the market-shed to find a cab.

***

Wednesday   22 September 1852 - London - Bethnal Green Cut

Olivier Ledouin had returned to London, and to the persona of Octavius Luker, only hours after sending his letters to the two representatives of the Paris police. He now sat in his third-floor office, gathering his thoughts about the last few days in preparation for an expected visitor. He had dropped a letter in at the finance-house near Threadneedle Street, and awaited his client.

He heard the familiar heavy tread on the stairs, and went to the door. His client hauled himself on to the landing and stood, breathing deeply. When he was able to speak, it was to say: "Your stairs are getting no easier, Luker." He walked through to sit in the leather chair. "Let us proceed to business."

Luker sat down opposite him. "I am sorry that I felt it necessary to disrupt your day, sir. It is only forty-eight hours since I wrote to you from Paris."

The other man drew a letter from a pocket inside his coat. "Aye, you told me that this Rougemont fellow had gone missing. Have you found him now?"

"Not in the condition that I would have wished, sir. The young man is dead. He was found in one of the canals in Paris. The circumstances of his death are suspicious, to say the least."

"Are you telling me that the man was murdered?"

"That is my belief. I felt that I should let you know as much without delay."

"And this is the fellow who was host to Franklin Blake and his wife, and whom you intended to persuade to leave Paris for Italy?"

"Indeed. Perhaps if I had succeeded in seeing him again sooner, he might by now have travelled south and be out of harm's way." He straightened some papers on his desk. "I have that young man on my conscience, sir." Luker's face was troubled.

There was silence in the room for several seconds. "I will own, Luker, that my mind begins to misgive me in this matter. It is working out in ways that I had not foreseen." He paused. "And would not have wished." He brought his fist down on the arm of his chair. "No, disgrace was what I wanted from the affair for Blake, not these deaths." He fell silent again.

"I sought this interview with you, sir, because I need to seek your guidance on what I should now do. I learnt while in Paris that Mr Blake is most likely to stand trial for the murder of the actress at the tavern. There may be no connection between that murder and the death of Louis Rougemont, but I cannot bring myself to believe that. And if there is a connection, then the fact that Monsieur Rougemont lost his life four days after Mr Blake was imprisoned, and possibly at the hands of a third party, throws a new light on the case against Mr Blake." He looked at his client. "Should I play any further role in the affair?"

"Do you have brandy in these infernal rooms?" It was not the response that Luker had expected, but he did indeed have a bottle in a cabinet against the wall, and he poured a glass for his client who took it hastily and drank. "Luker, I have resolved to offer you certain confidences. I expect you to lock them away in your head, and share them with no-one." The glass was raised, and more of the brandy drunk. "I am an old man, Luker, and have been married for many years, and happily married too. But now, my wife --" He broke off and drained the glass.

"I have kept my name from you so far. I shall tell it you now. Ablewhite. You have heard the name before. I am the father of Godfrey Ablewhite, the young man who perished three years ago. Since then, I have had to watch as Rachel Verinder, who jilted my son, entered into marriage with Franklin Blake, to watch as the two of them raised their good fortune up out of the ashes of my son's demise!" He held out the glass towards Luker, who refilled it. "A year ago, I knew that I could no longer sit idly by. With your help, I found a way to cast into their lives the shadows that have filled mine since Godfrey's death.

"But you must know that I acted without the knowledge of my wife. She is aunt to Rachel Blake, and has retained an affection for her which shows, alas, that her heart is stronger than her head. Aye, a creature of the heart, and I love her for it -- save in this regard!

"At the weekend, my wife was apprised of the scandal that has overtaken Franklin Blake. I wish that she had been spared the knowledge, but she received a letter from an accursed interfering relative who could find no better way to spend her time than to shatter my poor wife's ignorance. Do you have a family, Luker?" The agent shook his head. "Fortunate man! At all events, since receiving that letter my wife has had but one tune to sing. 'My poor suffering niece. We must find some way to help her.' Aye, all heart and no head!" He fell silent again.

After a few moments, Luker felt compelled to speak. "Your wife's compassion does her credit, sir."

"It may do, Luker, but it causes me a considerable headache. It was all I could do to dissuade my wife from rushing off to Paris immediately. I have had to undertake that I shall take steps to assist Mrs Blake!" It was said with distaste. "Though I have learnt that she has herself returned to Paris, with that leach of a lawyer, Bruff. Well, be that as it may, I had hoped to hear from you, Luker, and was glad of your note today. I must consult you on what I, or rather you, can do to make good on my undertaking to my wife."

"As to that, sir, I hope you may think that I have already made some small contribution."

"What's that?"

"Yesterday, before I left Paris, I sent letters to the police concerned with Monsieur Rougemont's death, to convey information relevant both to that young man's fate, and to the earlier demise of the actress which was the cause of Mr Blake's arrest."

Ablewhite gave him a look which was at one and the same time challenging and sympathetic. "I take it this was your conscience at work?" Luker nodded. "And do you think that the information will help Blake and his wife?"

"It may well do, if it is taken seriously by the police."

"Do you doubt their efficacy?"

Luker paused. "Not all the agents of the Paris police are cut from the same cloth. But I hope that the officer to whom I wrote at length is made of the right material to pursue the case effectively."

Ablewhite considered this. "You have not disclosed my identity to this officer, Luker?"

The other man smiled briefly. "Even if you had told me your name before today, sir, I would not have communicated it. Nor indeed have I given him my own name."

"Good. Is there more you can do in the matter while maintaining these confidences?"

It had always been a self-imposed rule for Luker that he should never turn down a client's request, so long as it was reasonable and largely within the bounds of legality. He would need to reflect at length about any further steps he could take: he was certain to think of something. "I am sure there is, sir. Do you instruct me to proceed?"

"Aye, Luker, proceed. I shall not ask after your methods, but bring about the result that my wife wishes to see -- though, heaven knows, it is not the outcome that I looked for only a week ago -- and you will not find me ungrateful." He stood up, took an envelope from his pocket, and set it down on Luker's desk. "That should keep you afloat for the present. Write to me as necessary, though I doubt not that Mrs Ablewhite will keep me informed of any developments."

He walked to the door, followed by the investigation agent. "Families -- comfort and turmoil in equal measure." Saying no more, he descended to the street and was gone. Luker retreated into his office.

Chapter Eleven
Wednesday 22 September 1852 - Paris - Rue de Calais

Boizillac's previous, and first, visit to the *Auberge des Dunes* had been in the evening, when darkness had hidden the dirt in the corners of the tavern and reflections of the burning candles had glittered in the bottles and glasses around the inn. Now, as he looked round the place in the cold light of day, he saw the muddy footprints on the floor and the scuffs and scratches on the walls that he had missed before. It felt less like a *salon* and more like a drinking-shop.

There was no sign of the landlord. With Delourcq alongside him, Boizillac went over to the bar, where the hefty young waiter stood. "I want to speak to Ricord."

The young man blinked. His reply, when it came after several seconds, was simply: "Why?"

"I am Captain Boizillac of the Sûreté." The waiter stared blankly at him. "I am a police agent."

"Another one?"

"What do you mean?"

"Ricord is in there, talking to him." He nodded towards the private room.

"Graize?" Delourcq commented. "This will be interesting."

As if summoned by his own name, the door to the room opened and Graize stepped out, only to stop at the sight of the others. "Boizillac? Are you still meddling in my investigation?"

"If you mean the death of Suzanne Pâquerette, no. I am here because of the murder of Louis Rougemont."

Graize's face darkened. "Rougemont? What concern is he to you?"

"Yesterday I received a letter from the man who acted as Rougemont's paymaster over the last few months." He took the letter from an inside pocket. "It led me to several discoveries, and it might be opportune for me to discuss them with you."

There was cold rage in Graize's eyes, but he spoke slowly and calmly. "Very well." He turned to the man behind him in the room. "Ricord, I need this room to talk to Monsieur Boizillac. We must not be disturbed." The landlord emerged, looking even more sullen than usual. "Go about your business without troubling us." Graize gave a peremptory wave to Boizillac. "Come. But we do not need him." Delourcq, to whom Graize referred, gave Boizillac a look of understanding. The younger man went into the room with the other policeman.

He sat down. Graize remained on his feet, looming above the table. "Your involvement in these cases is tiresome, Boizillac."

"I could not ignore a letter I was sent."

"Show it to me." Boizillac pushed it across the table, and watched as Graize scanned it, then put it in one of his own pockets. "As the man says, he wrote to me as well. There is little in his letter to you that I did not already know."

"But you wish to keep that letter?"

"Yes. This is my investigation, Boizillac."

"Into Rougemont's death?" Graize nodded. "And what have you found out?"

The other man gripped the back of the chair in front of him: his knuckles gleamed white. "I am content to hear what you have done, Boizillac. I have no intention of discussing my own investigations." He paused. "What have you done since receiving this letter?"

"I happened to learn the name of a man who may have been the other party to the meeting here, last Friday, when Rougemont agreed the sale of this precious stone. One Charles Rasquin. Is his name known to you?"

"It is, though I have not seen the man for some time."

"I saw him earlier today, at the Marché des Innocents."
He paused.

Graize tightened his grip on the chair even more.
"Rasquin is a blowhard and a fool. What did he say?"

"I asked him if he ever visited this tavern. He said he
did. Then I asked him if he came here last Friday and
met Rougemont. His only answer was that I should ask
the landlord, because his own recollection was not
clear. That is why I came here today, to question
Ricord. The only other thing that Rasquin said, several
times, was that he has the support of the Prince-
President's closest associates."

Graize cursed under his breath, and sat down at the
table abruptly. In silence, he read again the letter that
he had taken from Boizillac. Then, pushing his chair
back, he looked at the other man. "Your meddling
forces me after all to tell you what I have established,
Boizillac, but let this be an end to your interest in these
cases. Do I make myself clear?"

"As ever."

"Rasquin was here last Friday. He met Rougemont and
agreed to buy the stone from him. Rougemont handed
the stone over two days later, on Sunday. He was killed
later that evening. But it was not at Rasquin's hand that
he met his death."

"How do you know that?"

Graize's eyes blazed again, but he controlled his anger. "Much of Rasquin's prating is nonsense. But he does have a protector at the highest levels of government. My information comes from that source."

The remark hung in the air: both men had their own thoughts about the readiness of the regime to tolerate such creatures. Then Boizillac spoke. "So be it. But what of Ricord?"

"He has also told me that Rasquin was here last Friday."

"Do you trust Ricord?"

"I told you, Boizillac, it was from the highest level that I learnt that Rasquin was here. Ricord merely confirmed what I already knew. He allowed the two men to use this room for their discussion. They talked in private for half an hour, and then went their own ways."

"Last Wednesday, when the woman was killed, Ricord claimed that there was only one key to that store-room." Boizillac pointed to the door on the inner wall. "Yet the author of the letter you have taken from me tells us that the serving-man has a second key. Have you asked Ricord about that?"

"Do not waste any more of my time, or your own, on the murder of that woman. We have the killer. His name is Franklin Blake, and he will stand trial and, I doubt not, be found guilty."

"My question goes to the case of Rougemont. If the serving-man has a key to the store-room, could he have been in there while Rougemont and Rasquin were agreeing terms? Could he have heard where payment was to change hands, and decided to ambush Rougemont?"

"You think that the serving-man murdered Rougemont?"

"Do you have his killer?"

"Damn your insolence, Boizillac!" Graize got to his feet and loomed across the table. "And damn the man who wrote to you. He told you about the second key. He did not tell me!" He took the letter from his pocket, crumpled it into a ball, and hurled it on to the floor. "You will see how I can act when I have the information I need." He opened the door to the tavern. There were drinkers, but neither the landlord nor the serving-man were in evidence. "Get your man in here." Boizillac beckoned to Delourcq, who got up from a table by the window and went into the private room. "I shall find Ricord. Stay here till I come back." He stepped into the tavern and slammed the door shut behind him.

"In his usual good temper," said Delourcq. He sat down at the table.

"He already knew that it was Rasquin who met Rougemont here last Friday, but also that Rasquin was not the man's killer. And he's been told that by the highest authority - Rasquin is well connected."

"Like the gutter is connected to the sewer. It all stinks," the older man responded in a low growl.

"But what Monsieur L didn't tell him, though he did tell me, was that Ricord's serving-man has a second key to the store-room. That seemed to sting him into action."

Delourcq noticed the crumpled letter on the floor, and picked it up. "Did he do this?"

Boizillac nodded and took the letter back. "He went to speak to the landlord."

The other man gave a short laugh. "They should get on like a house on fire. I watched Ricord after he came out of talking to Graize. If looks could kill, all his customers would be dead by now. God knows why anyone chooses to drink here." The conversation paused for a few seconds, then Delourcq spoke again. "Odd, isn't it, captain?"

"What?"

"This Monsieur L telling you things he kept back from Graize. Do you think he'd met him and took as much of a dislike to him as everyone else?"

But before Boizillac could respond, the door opened again and the landlord came in, followed very closely by Graize. Ricord sat at the table, facing the other two men. Graize walked to stand behind them, and spoke over their heads. "Monsieur Boizillac has learnt that your serving-man has a second key to this store-room."

Ricord looked at Boizillac with scarcely concealed contempt. "What of it?"

The younger man was about to reply, but Graize's angry bark cut across him. "Last week, when the woman was killed here, you said there was only one key, and you held it. Explain yourself!"

Now the landlord's gaze shifted to Graize. There was scorn in his voice, but also an echo of the other man's wrath. "Émile was not serving here that night. As you may recall. So I did hold the only key."

"Where was he?"

"He said he had to help his political friends. I didn't ask any more about it."

"And where was he on Sunday night?" Graize asked.

There was a pause. "I don't know."

"With his political friends?"

Again, a pause. "He went out of his room here in the early evening and came back only on Monday morning."

"And you said nothing to him?"

"I said a good deal, and most of it was curses! But he kept his mouth shut."

"You should have told me this before, Ricord," Graize growled. "We know that Rougemont was in this room on Friday, when he met Rasquin and agreed arrangements for handing over a precious stone. If your serving-man was in that store-room, he could have overheard what they agreed. You now say that the man was away from the tavern on Sunday evening, when Rougemont was killed. So answer this question - where was he when Rougemont and Rasquin met here last Friday?"

Ricord looked at Graize. "I sent him to get some more bread for the kitchen." His gaze flickered. "But -- he could have been in the store-room. He was very slow in re-appearing."

"If I find that you have kept anything else back from me, Ricord, I shall close this place down!" Graize's face was full of fury. With a visible effort, he spoke to the other police agent. "Boizillac, I thank you for your help. Now that this apology for a landlord has finally given me the full story, I have little doubt about the culpability of his serving-man. Where is he, Ricord?"

"He was behind the bar when you brought me in here."

Graize went through, followed by Ricord. But Émile was gone. Urged on by Graize, the landlord led the policeman up the stairs at the back of the tavern, to the small attic room where the serving-man spent his nights. Only a couple of minutes later, the two of them clattered back to the ground floor, to find Boizillac and Delourcq standing by the bar, waiting for them.

"Not there", said Graize, in a voice thick with anger. "And if running away wasn't enough to prove his guilt, this settles it." He held out a small, drawstring bag. "He was in such a hurry to go that he left this under his mattress. There's more money in here than the villain would earn in a year."

"You think he took it from Rougemont?" Boizillac asked.

"Where else?" Graize responded curtly. He turned to Ricord, who stood sullenly behind him. "He was working for you. Did you give him this money?" Ricord shook his head. "Did he ever have money before?"

"No. All he had in his pockets were the scraps of bread left on the tables." It was said with a sneer.

"Shame the landlord didn't feed him better," said Delourcq under his breath.

"Where is he likely to run to?" Graize threw the question at Ricord.

"Can't say. What family he has live in Normandy. His friends in Paris? Who knows?"

"If he comes creeping back here, send me word at once, Ricord. Otherwise there'll be a price for you to pay." The air between the two men seemed full of venom. Without a further word, the landlord moved off to deal with his customers. "Good day, Boizillac. I have a search to organise. And you have other work to concern you. We are agreed?" With a final, meaningful look at the younger man, Graize strode out of the tavern.

"It seems there's nothing more for us to do here, Delourcq." The two men left as well. Ricord followed them to the door, watched as they made their way along the road, then slammed the door shut muttering a curse that took in all three of the police agents, his serving-man and the remaining drinkers. How long could he keep the tavern going in the midst of so much scandal?

***

Wednesday 22 September 1852 - Paris - Rue du Bac

It was dark when Boizillac climbed the stairs to his lodgings in the Rue du Bac. He and Delourcq had spent the rest of the day dealing with what Graize had called their other work. Boizillac looked forward to regaining the peace of mind he always found when he and Laure were in each other's company. Laure was not on-stage tonight, and she had promised to spend the evening alone with him.

But it was not to be. As he let himself into his rooms, Laure came to meet him, holding a candle. "I have brought an old friend to see you, Lucien."

Another young woman appeared, did an exaggerated curtsey, and spoke theatrically: "Monsieur de Boizillac, I am delighted to see you again after such a long time."

She was Delphine Ramille. When Boizillac had got to know Laure, a year before, she and Delphine were acting in the same production; off-stage, they were often together as well; and their first meeting was *à quatre*, a supper arranged by a fellow former soldier, Nicolas de Montholon. Delphine's friendship with Montholon had been intense, but short-lived; and Montholon, who had also lodged in the house in the Rue du Bac, had since left Paris to seek his fortune in North Africa. The two young women had gone their separate ways, and had not seen each other since the turn of the year.

Lucien glanced at Laure, and then replied: "Not so long, Delphine. You haven't changed at all."

"Why, thank you, kind sir." She laughed loudly, and shook her blonde hair. "And you are as elegant as ever. Oh how I envy Laure her good fortune!"

Laure blushed slightly. "Please behave yourself, Delphine." It was said with a mixture of affection and mild rebuke. "You wanted to speak to Lucien on a serious matter. But come, we must let Lucien sit down." She took his coat from him, gently stroking his cheek as she did so.

They had a plain wooden table and two chairs in the main room of the lodgings, as well as an armchair that had seen better days. When they were alone, Boizillac would sit in the armchair and cradle Laure on his lap. Now, the two women sat at either side of the table, leaving Lucien to take sole possession of his favourite seat. "Are you in trouble, Delphine?" he asked.

There was a peal of laughter in reply. "Me? Why no. I have any number of elderly admirers who are determined to supplement what I earn in the *Théâtre Parisien*, and I always respect the wishes of my elders. And my theatrical career has never been more successful, even though I no longer share the stage with my dear Laure." She checked herself. "All was perfect, until a week ago." She looked at Boizillac. "When my other dear friend, Suzanne Pâquerette, was killed."

Boizillac sat upright. "You knew Suzanne Pâquerette?"

Delphine was momentarily overcome by the memory, and her eyes filled with tears. "Yes, Lucien," Laure said, "Delphine was acting in the same play. But there was no performance last Wednesday, and the production has been closed since."

Boizillac had talked privately to Laure about the case, but neither of them had realised that Delphine had been connected with the dead woman. "I am sorry. But why did you want to speak to me?"

She dabbed her eyes with a lace handkerchief that she took from a small reticule. "She told me about her meeting that night, how she was going to confront the Englishman. She spoke bitterly about him."

"It seems that he abandoned her some years ago."

Delphine leaned forward on her chair. "But she suffered an even greater betrayal. She often spoke to me about that, too." Now her eyes gleamed. "Many men courted Suzanne, men of business, men of politics. She knew how to keep them at a distance, without driving them away completely. But there was one man she prized above all of them - as did most of France." She paused, savouring the moment.

"One man?" Boizillac repeated, not fully understanding.

Delphine got to her feet, struck a triumphal pose, and fluttered her hands on either side of her top lip, and below her chin, as though she was preening a moustache and beard. "A man of destiny," she intoned.

"The Prince-President? And Suzanne Pâquerette?" Boizillac knew of the man's fondness for actresses, but this was a startling revelation. "Did you ever see them together?"

"No, they were very discreet. But Suzanne left me in no doubt. And here is the proof." With a flourish, she pulled a folded letter from her handbag and gave it to Boizillac.

He read it through.

"My much-loved Suzanne. If only we could share all our nights. If only I could hold your body to mine all the time, and feel your warmth, your softness, your beauty tremble beneath me. Believe that my heart is yours entirely, and do not reproach me for the company of other women. Their charms are nothing compared with yours. Yes, even this young Spanish woman, Eugénie, who won such praise at the reception this

month - she is but an arid desert compared to the lush landscape of your body. Keep me in your heart until you hold me in your arms again."

It was dated April 1849, and signed C-L N. He read the initials out loud.

Delphine paused, then said: "Charles-Louis Napoléon. And Eugénie is the woman that all Paris now expects him to marry."

"1849," Boizillac said. "Three years ago."

"But their *liaison* continued until the start of this summer. Then, after three years when she gave him all her love and devotion, he threw her over and said that his future meant that he had to break with his past."

Boizillac thought of the preparations that were being made for the return of the Empire. The story was plausible, and yet: "You have no letters of more recent date?"

"There were many of them, believe me, Lucien. But the day after my poor Suzanne was killed, they were all taken from her lodgings."

"By whom?"

"A police inspector. He turned up, saying that he wanted to check whether this Englishman had written to Suzanne. When he left, all her letters went with him."

"And this one?"

205

"Suzanne always kept it in the gown that she wore on stage, as a sort of lucky charm. I'd forgotten about it until today. I was at the theatre today, thinking about her, and I pulled the gown on to feel nearer to her." She mimicked the action, hugging a robe against herself. "And I found the letter."

"The police inspector. Do you know his name?"

"I wasn't there when he came. But the *concierge* said he was a tall man, with a big black beard, and a manner like a bear with a sore head."

"Graize," Boizillac murmured. "Why did you want to tell me about this, Delphine?"

She sat down again and looked at the floor for a moment. "I don't know." Then her eyes flashed as she looked up. "Suzanne was so badly treated by that man. She passed word that he should make amends to her, or she would make sure that his letters became common knowledge." She started to weep. "And now she's dead, and all her letters are gone, except for that one, and I just wanted someone else to know, someone who understands what is happening --" She covered her face. Laure knelt down next to her and comforted her.

Boizillac sat, staring at the letter, and gathering his thoughts. It was five years since the affair between Suzanne Pâquerette and the Englishman had ended; her *liaison* with the Prince-President had begun after that and finished, it seemed, only months before. If she had been filled with resentment at this most recent abandonment, could she have re-directed it towards Franklin Blake when he unknowingly crossed her path again? Could her sense of grievance have led her to provoke the Englishman so harshly that he was driven to attack her? Was it even possible that Blake knew about her involvement with the Prince-President and taunted her about it? His head was suddenly full of questions that seemed unanswerable.

Delphine got to her feet; there were tears still in her eyes, but she dabbed at them and smiled. "Well, now that I have told you my story, I must leave."

Laure took her hand. "No, you can't leave like this, Delphine. Can she, Lucien?" Boizillac shook his head in agreement. "Sit down again. I will find something for us to eat. And you will sleep here tonight."

"Oh, but Laure, two are company, three are none."

"And a friend in need is a friend indeed." Now Laure came and put her hand on Boizillac's shoulder. "You don't mind, do you?"

"No, no," he said. "You must be our guest."

Delphine clapped her hands in delight, and the two young women set about preparing food. It was not the evening that Boizillac had expected; he was occasionally diverted by the pleasure that Laure and Delphine took in bringing each other up-to-date; but, even as their chatter helped the evening slip past, his mind was filled with speculation about Suzanne Pâquerette and her male suitors.

Chapter Twelve

It was only twenty-four hours since the two men had last met. Graize had asked to see Persigny urgently, and now they faced each other across the Minister's desk.

"My time is limited," Persigny said. "Has a difficulty arisen?"

Graize shifted on his chair, which constricted his large frame. "I have established the identity of the man who murdered Louis Rougemont." The other man waited for the explanation to be completed. "Émile Leboeuf."

"I have seen that name somewhere."

"Leboeuf was the serving-man at the *Auberge des Dunes*. He worked for Ricord."

Persigny leaned forward, across the desk, towards Graize. "Ricord's man? How was he involved?"

"He overheard the conversation between Rougemont and Rasquin." A look of disdain appeared briefly on Graize's face. "He ambushed Rougemont after he had been paid, took his money, and killed him."

"He acted alone?"

Graize considered his answer for a second or two. "You mean Ricord? He has told me he had no hand in Rougemont's killing. I have taken his word, for the moment. As for any others, I shall ask Leboeuf when I find him."

"You've not arrested him?" Persigny asked.

"He ran away from the tavern moments before I could do so. But I will find him. Leboeuf is strong, but stupid. I will find him before the day is out."

"Make sure you do, and lock him up immediately."

Graize raised his hand in a scarcely concealed gesture of impatience. "I know what to do about Leboeuf. You need not worry."

Persigny took it badly. "It is not your place to tell me whether to worry or not. Do you think that I would be in this office today, or that we would have a Bonaparte as our Prince-President, if I had not spent year after year worrying, as you call it!" The words rang around the room, and several seconds passed until the succeeding silence was broken. "Very well, Graize, I know of your abilities. I am sure I can rely on you in this as well."

"I asked to see you today not just to tell you about Leboeuf's crime, but about the way in which it was revealed - and by whom." Graize's hands rested on his knees; now they folded into fists, clenched in anger. "Boizillac. Captain Lucien de Boizillac, of the Sûreté. He blundered into the *Auberge des Dunes* a week ago, when the woman was killed. He followed Rougemont back to his house and questioned him about the Englishman. And he learnt that Leboeuf had his own keys for all the doors in the tavern, and could have eavesdropped on Rougemont's meeting with Rasquin. Boizillac came to the *Auberge des Dunes* yesterday, when I was with Ricord. He told me what he had learnt. It was clear that Leboeuf had to be arrested." Graize flexed his fingers, then pressed one fist into the palm of his other hand. "I have told him to leave these matters alone. His interest is unnecessary, and unwelcome!"

"Boizillac?" Persigny asked. "But it was Boizillac who investigated the killings that led to the murder of General Vauzuron last year." He thought for a moment. "Are you confident that he will do as you asked?"

Graize's expression darkened. "No. I cannot understand the man. He seems only too happy to tread on other people's feet." His eyes narrowed. "They may end up kicking him hard."

Persigny raised one of his hands. "There should be no need for that. I know about Boizillac. There are levers that I can pull to see that he pursues his interest no further. Leave that to me." He stood up; the other man

211

did so as well. "Get hold of Leboeuf as soon as possible, Graize. He cannot be allowed to remain at liberty. As for Ricord -- you know your man. But we must be sure that we are building on solid foundations. If there is any weakness about Ricord, we cannot rely on him."

Graize's response was a curt "Your servant". He left the office. Persigny returned to his desk to write a letter, for immediate transmission.

***

Thursday 23 September - afternoon - Hotel Bristol, Place Vendôme

Matthew Bruff sat in the foyer of the hotel, a cup of coffee on the table in front of him. He found himself staring at the steaming liquid, seeing in its impenetrable blackness a sign of the prospects for Rachel Blake and, more ominously, her husband. Earlier that day, he had gone with her to visit Franklin Blake in his imprisonment; and although both the visitors had done their best to encourage optimism, Blake's spirits had been at a very low ebb. A week behind bars would oppress any man, thought Bruff; and a man of so mercurial a temper as Blake could easily fall into deeper gloom than most.

He was jolted from these thoughts by a soft voice. "Mr Matthew Bruff?"

He looked up. A figure stood before him, holding a hat in both hands, with an expression of respect on his face. "That is my name. And yours?"

The other man gave a flicker of a smile. "I am known as Olivier Ledouin, sir. I would be glad of a word with you."

Bruff had now fixed his gaze firmly on him. "A French name. Your English is impeccable." He paused. "What word do you have in mind?"

Ledouin glanced around the foyer. "Might I be so bold as to sit with you, sir? I had rather not broadcast my words."

"You strike a mysterious tone, Monsieur Ledouin. But sit down, by all means. And tell me how you know who I am."

Ledouin took a chair opposite Bruff, leaning forward, so that he was required to look up towards the other man's face. "I am often in London, sir, and know of your standing in that city's legal profession."

"I cannot recall that we have met, however. What is your business in London?"

"It is generally of a confidential nature." There was silence for a moment or two. "I carry out investigations, in a private capacity, for a number of clients."

"Indeed? Well, each man must come to terms with how he earns his living. But I fail to see what purpose someone in your position would wish to serve by approaching me." He took a large mouthful of coffee and swallowed it quickly.

"Forgive me, Mr Bruff, I owe you an explanation. This is not a chance meeting. I have expressly sought you out."

Bruff had begun to drum his fingers on the table. There was distaste in his voice when he spoke again. "Monsieur Ledouin, I give you five minutes. I am not habituated to striking up conversations with unknown individuals whose work consists of prying into the affairs of others. If your explanation fails to answer, this interview will end promptly in five minutes' time."

Ledouin touched his brow with his right hand. "Sir, my approach concerns Franklin Blake."

"Be damned if it does!"

"I know that Mr Blake is being held in prison pending trial, and that you have come here as the family lawyer. I have information about the circumstances which led to his arrest, that I wish to provide to you."

"Have you, indeed? And how came you by this information?"

"Allow me to explain." Ledouin composed himself. "For some time, I have been acting on behalf of a client whose purpose was to bring Mr Blake into disrepute."

214

The other man bridled. "The devil! Who is this client?"

Ledouin raised both his hands. "I cannot disclose his name, sir, but I can tell you that he now regrets his actions and has asked me to do what I can to redress the harm done."

"This is a very shabby story, Monsieur Ledouin." Bruff stared furiously at the investigation agent.

"I do not seek to deny it, sir. Will you allow me to continue?" Bruff flicked his right hand at Ledouin, to indicate assent. "Louis Rougemont invited Mr and Mrs Blake to Paris under my instruction, at my client's behest. I had previously agreed with Suzanne Pâquerette that she would confront Mr Blake once he was in this city, and, as you know, she did so a week ago, with fatal consequences."

Bruff was drumming the table again. "If what you say is true, Monsieur Ledouin, you and your client have practised a monstrous deceit on Franklin Blake and his wife." He rested his hands. "But what proof have you of the truth of your story?"

Ledouin placed a piece of paper on the table. As Bruff picked it up, he noted the date of 1847, and the acknowledgement that the writer bore a debt of 1,000 French francs for a loan made by Jean-Marie Ricord, of the *Auberge des Dunes*. It was written and signed by Franklin Blake. The lawyer looked at Ledouin. "I have seen this before, among the papers of the late Julia Verinder. How did it enter into your possession?"

"Another detail which I must withhold, sir. But I hope that this shows my *bona fides*."

"Your choice of words provokes me, Monsieur Ledouin, it provokes me mightily. But the document persuades me that our interview should continue. Explain to me how you see a way to undo the damage that your infamous plotting has caused."

"It turns, sir, on the *Auberge des Dunes*. Mademoiselle Pâquerette asked Mr Blake to meet her there at my suggestion, because I had already secured the co-operation of the tavern-keeper in the arrangements that I had made."

"Ricord?"

"The very same, sir."

"I take it that he received payment from you? And he knew in advance that Mr Blake and the actress would meet that evening at his tavern?"

"He did. He was still hostile towards Mr Blake because of his slowness in paying back the loan, and this hostility, together with the sum that I gave him, disposed him very readily to allow his tavern to be used for the encounter." For a moment, Ledouin studied the hat he held on his lap.

"You wish to say more about the man?" Bruff prompted.

"Only this, sir. If we assume that Mademoiselle Pâquerette did not die at the hands of Mr Blake --"

"Unthinkable!"

"-- then a third person must have been the cause of her death. And it might be supposed that Ricord would have some knowledge of such a person."

"Hold, Monsieur Ledouin, while I follow your drift. Are you suggesting that Ricord himself was the perpetrator?"

"No, sir, he was not. He was seen in his tavern throughout the time when Mr Blake and Mademoiselle Pâquerette were meeting in private."

"Conclusive as to his own activities. But he may have colluded with yet another who struck the dreadful blows?" The investigation agent said nothing. "Monsieur Ledouin, for a man who wishes to provide information you can be remarkably silent. Speak up if there is more detail."

"Ricord has employed a serving-man, Émile Leboeuf. But on the fateful night he was not seen on serving duties in the tavern. I can offer you no more than that, and a nagging doubt in my mind that Ricord and his man may know the truth of Mademoiselle Pâquerette's demise."

Bruff waited several seconds, resting his gaze on the other man. Then: "This has been an interview which I would far rather have avoided, Monsieur Ledouin. I burn with anger to learn that you and your client were responsible for laying the snare which now holds Franklin Blake fast." He inhaled deeply. "But perhaps your contrition, though late in the day, has come in good time to help Franklin from it. I have your account perfectly in my head, and I shall at once go to Maître Denonvilliers, who will defend Franklin, to repeat it. For your contrition and information, I thank you. For the rest -- I have said enough!" He stood up and gave the briefest of nods to Ledouin, who also rose, bowed to the other man, and left the hotel without delay.

***

Thursday 23 September - early evening - Paris - Prefecture of Police

Boizillac had spent the day on other matters, following up possible leads on the whereabouts of Cotte and others suspected of anti-government agitation, but his mind had been full of what Delphine had told him about Suzanne Pâquerette. What had really happened in that room at the *Auberge des Dunes*? And could he really let go of the case and leave it to Graize?

He had an inkling that the appointment he was now waiting to keep might answer these questions. It was six o'clock. He stood in the street outside the main entrance to the Prefecture, as he had been asked to do in the sealed letter that had been delivered to him earlier in the afternoon, by a *sergent de ville* sent out to find him.

218

One glance at the seal told him that it was from his half-brother, the Duc de Morny. The letter itself contained no more than a request for the meeting, and an assurance that it was of the highest importance.

They had met only once before, on the day of the *coup* the previous December when the Prince-President had seized control of France. Morny had shocked Boizillac to the core then, as much by his revelation of their kinship as by his suppression of the younger man's murder investigations, in the national interest. Neither man had sought to deepen their acquaintance since. Boizillac had carried on his work for the Sûreté, accepting that the arrest of anti-Bonapartists was the price to be paid for protecting Laure and her family. And within two months of the *coup*, Morny had left his role as Minister of the Interior to expand his business interests and make money from investing in the new companies that were spreading the railways across France.

A carriage appeared. The driver stopped the horses. The door opened, and Charles de Morny waved to Boizillac. He got in, and the carriage moved off again.

Morny was ten years older than Boizillac, and much the same age as the Prince-President. He might have been mistaken for the latter: they both had the same receding hair-line, and the same prominent moustache and beard. But Boizillac saw little of his own appearance in Morny; he accepted that they had the same father, in the Comte de Flahaut, but he felt no emotional ties to this man.

"Lucien," Morny began. "I should not have neglected you all these months. But business is a jealous mistress, you know: it is difficult to escape her attentions."

"Monsieur de Morny."

The other man nodded. "Short, and to the point. Well, perhaps you are right. We cannot pretend that we are a close-knit family. But you are well?"

"Thank you."

"And thank you for accepting my invitation to see you today. I am no longer a member of the Government, but it seems that I have not been entirely forgotten by it." He smiled. "I passed charge of my Ministry to the Vicomte de Persigny. He contacted me earlier today, and it was at his instigation that I asked to see you, Lucien."

"I have not met Monsieur de Persigny."

"That is no great loss," Morny sighed. "At all events, Persigny thinks that I have influence with you, and he has asked me to exercise it in relation to a certain matter. You may have some idea of what that is."

"The killings of Suzanne Pâquerette and Louis Rougemont?"

"Exactly." Morny took a letter from his coat pocket. "Persigny has written to me at great length about the cases. But the nub of it is that the police inspector in charge of the investigations has established who was responsible for the murders, that the guilty parties will face justice very soon, and that your continued involvement is unnecessary and undesirable." He looked at Boizillac. "I will not pretend that I agree with Persigny in all matters, but I take his letter very seriously, Lucien, and I advise you to do so too."

Boizillac reflected on what he had been told. Graize was leaving no stone unturned to ensure that he remained in sole control of the case. But to get the Minister to intervene suggested that there was more to it than Graize's well-known misanthropy. "How much do you know about the murders?" he asked.

"The Englishman, Blake, stands accused of killing the woman, who was threatening to tarnish his good name, at this tavern, the *Auberge des Dunes*. His friend, Rougemont, was robbed and murdered by the serving-man from the tavern after he had received money in exchange for a precious stone. Squalid crimes, but Persigny writes that the perpetrators are known, and that justice can now take its course."

"Justice," Boizillac repeated. "Does the Minister write that Blake, and all who know him well, say that he is incapable of such an act of violence? Does he have anything to say about Ricord, the landlord of the *Auberge des Dunes*, who claims to have had no idea of what his serving-man did?" He paused, and then went on. "And does he say anything about a *liaison* between Suzanne Pâquerette and the man we all serve -- the Prince-President?"

"I can see that you have taken a close interest in this case, Lucien." There was admiration in his voice. "Well, as for Mademoiselle Pâquerette, Persigny does acknowledge that she had been involved with Louis." It took Boizillac a second or two to realise that Morny was referring to the Prince-President. "But I knew that already. I saw him with her on several occasions, and it was clear that he savoured her charms. She was not the first actress to enjoy his attentions."

"But does the Minister also tell you that Suzanne Pâquerette had kept letters she had been sent by him, and that she threatened to make the letters public when he broke off their *liaison* earlier this year?"

The mood in the carriage had suddenly become more serious. "Do you have evidence of this?"

Boizillac had been carrying around with him the letter that Delphine passed to him the night before. Now he showed it to Morny. "I understand that there were many other letters, but they were taken from her lodgings after she had been killed, by the investigating police officer."

"Louis was unwise to write this," Morny said softly, almost to himself. "May I keep it?"

"Can you make use of it?" Morny nodded. "Then do so." Boizillac felt both regret, that he had given up such a salient document, and relief, a sense that, while he could take his investigation no further, perhaps his powerful half-brother might.

"What manner of man is this Blake?"

Boizillac thought for a moment. "He is about the same age as me, and has a young wife whom he clearly loves. I have met them both. Blake seems an honourable man, but his moods are at the mercy of circumstances. Of the two, his wife is the more impressive. She has enough resolve in her character for both of them."

"And she is certain that Blake did not kill the actress?" Morny asked. Boizillac nodded. "That is hardly surprising, for a devoted wife."

"It was also the firm belief of Rougemont, Blake's friend, who was still troubled by doubts when he went back to the tavern last Friday, to agree the sale of the precious stone."

"You saw Rougemont after that, before he was killed?"

"No, I was told of his doubts in a letter from Rougemont's sponsor here in Paris."

"Ah yes," Morny countered. "Persigny has mentioned that too. And he also says that the British Ambassador has written on Blake's behalf, pressing for the man's release. Did you know that, Lucien?" The other man shook his head. "Persigny has dismissed the suggestion out of hand. He has a visceral dislike for the British. Understandable if we were at war with them. Short-sighted in present times, when France can learn valuable lessons from them in matters of industry and commerce." He caught himself before he said any more.

223

"Lucien, I need to be sure that you will intervene no further in these cases. I have some credit with Persigny and his fellow Ministers, but that will be spent if I cannot persuade you today."

It was only his second meeting with his half-brother; as had happened before, he was being obliged to step back from an investigation. But this time he had all but reached the same conclusion before seeing Morny. He said as much to him, then: "But you will reflect on what I have told you, today, and on the letter to Suzanne Pâquerette which I gave you?"

"I shall. It will serve no-one's interest for the worst of the Prince-President's indiscretions to become public knowledge, and the letter will stay firmly in my possession. But you have shone more light on the picture that Persigny had painted for me. I give you my word that I shall think further about it. And I shall do urgently -- Persigny writes that the Englishman will be brought to trial tomorrow."

"Tomorrow?"

Morny nodded. He had a cane by his side, and now he used it to tap on the ceiling of the carriage, which was brought to a stop. "Are you happy to step down here?"

The carriage had been winding around the roads that fringed the Île du Palais. They were now back on the Quai des Orfèvres, only a stone's throw from the Prefecture. Boizillac moved to open the door.

"Thank you, Lucien. If you ever tire of police work, let me know. My companies are starting to grow, and there will be real opportunities for men such as you."

He paused. "I don't think that my path runs that way."

Morny smiled. "Perhaps not. Or at least, not yet. *Adieu*, Lucien."

Boizillac stepped down and closed the door. A fine drizzle was falling, and spray flew from the wheels of the disappearing carriage. He turned up his collar and walked in the opposite direction.

Chapter Thirteen
Friday 24 September 1852 - Paris

It was a day when the sky above the city saw the first flight of an airship. Henri Giffard succeeded in getting his dirigible into the air and steering it to Élancourt, a dozen or more miles away. To many of the Parisians who craned their necks to watch the flight, it seemed like a reflection of their country's ascent under the Prince-President.

For Franklin Blake, however, the day marked the latest stage in his slow and steady descent. He had received only a few hours' notice that he would be put on trial, when Maître Denonvilliers had come to his cell to talk to him. He had spent most of the period since pacing back and forth, trying for the umpteenth time to recall clearly all that had happened in the *Auberge des Dunes* that night. And then he had been escorted from his cell, to stand now in the courtroom, facing the three judges of the *cour d'assises* at one end, with Antoine Denonvilliers and Ferdinand Talabot, the prosecuting attorney, only a few steps away from him, court officials placed at desks and doors all around - and seats full of spectators in a gallery above.

Denonvilliers had described the scene in advance, but Blake had to make a continuous effort to resist the bewilderment that settled on him. He heard the presiding judge call the court to order; he heard him ask whether his name was Franklin Blake, whether he was English and whether his main place of residence was London; and he heard himself give a positive answer to all these questions. But, even after a week in prison, he struggled to believe that he had been brought here to face trial for the murder of the French actress; that this dark and vaulting room was the place where he might be found guilty of the crime; and that, if he were, he might never see the light of day again. He glanced up, towards the windows; his eyes took in the spectators above; and suddenly he saw his dear Rachel, staring fixedly at him. A look passed between them; it was as if Rachel was sending her energy to him; and Blake strengthened, and prepared for his ordeal.

Ferdinand Talabot opened proceedings. A short man, built like a barrel and draped in court finery, he had the style and swagger of a leading actor in the theatre. He fixed Aristide de Lavalette, the presiding judge, with a gaze that combined respect with authority. "Monsieur le Président," he intoned to the presiding judge, stretching the syllables to breaking-point, "the court will today hear the details of no ordinary crime, committed by no ordinary criminal. How many times has this court seen some brick-layer, or cart-driver, who has wasted his wages on an excess of cheap wine and then turned on his wife, or some woman of the night, only to beat her senseless?"

He paused, then looked at Blake. "Not today. The accused who stands before you today is neither brick-layer nor cart-driver, but an English *milord*." The word was spoken with distaste. "Mr Franklin Blake has the manners and the mien of a gentleman. But, as the court will hear, what transpired in the *Auberge des Dunes* in the evening of the fifteenth day of this month revealed that such manners, such a mien are only skin-deep -- and beneath them lies a streak of savagery needing only the lubricants of anger and alcohol to break out into the light of day.

"We shall show that in that tavern, on that evening, Franklin Blake took the life of Suzanne Pâquerette, an actress, with whom he had enjoyed a close friendship some four or five years ago -- a friendship that ended, and turned both parties against each other. It was Mademoiselle Pâquerette's misfortune to seek to renew that friendship. But it was Mr Blake's nemesis that he was overcome by a wine-fuelled fury, and that his hands fastened round the neck of his spurned lover and ended her life.

"It matters not whether a murderer is brick-layer or baron, he must atone for his crime. We shall show that Mr Blake committed this murder. And we shall press for him to pay the ultimate penalty." Talabot stood in silence while his words sank in. Then he resumed his place.

Franklin Blake felt his courage slipping away. Denonvilliers, getting to his feet, smiled briefly at him, then addressed the court in his turn. "Monsieur le Président, I agree with my learned colleague, Maître

Talabot, that we are dealing with no ordinary crime. But I part company with him when he seeks to attribute responsibility for that crime to Mr Franklin Blake.

"Mr Blake came to Paris earlier this month, not to seek out Mademoiselle Pâquerette, but to visit an old friend, Louis Rougemont, who had invited him to the city. It was Mademoiselle Pâquerette who instigated their rendez-vous at the *Auberge des Dunes* and, though Mr Blake kept that meeting with great reluctance, and with apprehension about the outcome, he made no secret of it to his wife. He had no fears about any disclosures that Suzanne Pâquerette might threaten to make. He had no reason to commit the murder. He did not do so.

"So how are we to explain her death that evening, and the circumstances in which she and Mr Blake were discovered? Your Honour, since Mr Blake is innocent, there must be another explanation, another perpetrator of this crime. Among those present in the courtroom today, there may be one or more individuals who know the truth of what happened in the *Auberge des Dunes* that evening. We shall seek for that explanation as we examine the witnesses, in the certainty that it was not Franklin Blake who brought the life of Mademoiselle Pâquerette to a sudden and violent end. And we shall press for Mr Blake to be exonerated, and allowed to walk free. I say to the court: *sapere aude*! Dare to be wise - we must all have the courage to apply wisdom in understanding what has happened." He sat down again.

As the spectators in the gallery muttered to one another about the opening speeches, the first witness was called. It was Graize, who took his place in a box opposite

Blake. He paid no attention to the Englishman; his eyes were fixed on the prosecuting attorney.

"Inspector Graize, you were the first to discover the crime," Talabot said. "Describe what you saw."

"It was in the evening of Wednesday of last week. I had gone to the *Auberge des Dunes* in order to speak to the landlord, Jean-Marie Ricord. I heard the sound of a commotion in a private room at the back of the tavern. I broke down the door, and found the woman, Suzanne Pâquerette lying dead on the floor. She had been strangled. A man lay on top of her, unconscious. It was that man, Franklin Blake. He was drunk, and incapable of speech."

"And there was no-one else in the private room?"

"Not when I entered. But I was followed by the landlord."

"Ricord? We shall take evidence from him as well. So the only people in that room were Mademoiselle Pâquerette, who had been murdered, and Franklin Blake. Is it your opinion that Mr Blake was the murderer?"

Graize's eyes blazed. "It is."

"Mr Blake denies committing the crime. Do you know of any reason why he would have done so?"

"There was a liaison between the two of them some years ago, when Blake was living in Paris. He returned to England and has since married. The woman Pâquerette threatened to expose details of their liaison. Put to death, she would be unable to do so."

"We have heard that Mr Blake had made no secret of that liaison to his wife. If so, would he still have had reason to end her life?"

Graize was emphatic in his reply. "Every reason! Confidences between man and wife remain in the bed-chamber. But a man - a *gentleman* - has a standing in society which may not survive the revelations of a former mistress. Blake had a choice - either the woman perished, or his reputation would do so!"

Talabot let the words hang in the air, then nodded an obeisance towards the judges, and sat down.

Denonvilliers rose. "Inspector Graize, Mr Franklin Blake is a gentleman who belongs to the highest echelons of English society. Do you really believe that a man of his calibre would be capable of so squalid a crime as to strangle an actress in a third-rate tavern?"

"By their deeds shall ye know them." Graize's voice rumbled like a preacher. "I know what I saw in the *Auberge des Dunes*. English gentleman he may be, but I saw him sprawled on top of a dead woman."

Denonvilliers paused. "But you did not see him attack Mademoiselle Pâquerette, did you?"

Graize bridled. "I heard an uproar only seconds before I broke down the door, and then I found Blake lying on top of the woman."

"You entered through the door that opened from the main room of the tavern. But was there another door into the private room?"

The policeman's look darkened. "There was a door at the back that gave on to a storage area. But it was locked."

"And who held a key to that second door?"

"Ricord, who followed me."

"And Émile Leboeuf, the serving-man?"

"Leboeuf?" Graize seemed to struggle with the name.

"Did Leboeuf have a key to the private room?" Denonvilliers waited a few seconds but, receiving no reply, went on. "Well, there will be an answer when he is called as a witness." For a moment, Graize's composure faltered. He gripped the wooden ledge that ran round the top of the box where he stood, and stared down at the floor. Denonvilliers spoke again. "Inspector Graize?" The policeman said something, too quietly to be understood. "Please speak up, Inspector Graize."

"Leboeuf is dead." He raised his head again and formed his words slowly, but deliberately. "He died yesterday, resisting arrest." The murmur among the spectators became louder.

"This is startling news. Why was Leboeuf being arrested?"

Ferdinand Talabot got to his feet and addressed the judge. "Monsieur le Président, we shall have cause to speak of Émile Leboeuf when his employer, Jean-Marie Ricord, gives evidence in this court. Might I propose that this witness be spared further questions about the serving-man?"

Denonvilliers was not ready to step back entirely. "I am content to defer further questions so long as Inspector Graize answers the question that I have already asked."

"So be it," the presiding judge responded. "Inspector Graize?"

"Leboeuf was being arrested -- for the murder of Louis Rougemont."

"Louis Rougemont?" echoed Denonvilliers. "The man who was host to Mr and Mrs Franklin Blake during their stay in Paris. The man who accompanied Mr Blake to the *Auberge des Dunes* on that fateful night. And the serving-man from that tavern was to be arrested for murdering Louis Rougemont. Well, I have no more to ask Inspector Graize now. But I would remind him of the motto that he enunciated: by their deeds shall ye know them."

Denonvilliers sat down. The policeman left the witness-box, to be replaced by the landlord of the *Auberge des Dunes*. Ricord had made some attempt to look respectable; he wore a long black frock-coat which, though it had seen better days, matched the sombreness of the court-room, and he was freshly shaven; but his eyes darted back and forth nervously, and his face had a look which married fear with contempt.

"Jean-Marie Ricord," Talabot began. "You are the landlord of the *Auberge des Dunes* in the Rue de Calais?"

"Yes."

"How long have you run the tavern?"

"Since 1842."

"So, ten years. Have there been difficulties with the law before?"

"No," Ricord shot back. "Well, one or two fights." He shrugged.

"Monsieur Ricord, we have heard from Inspector Graize about his discovery of Mr Blake and Mademoiselle Pâquerette in the private room in your tavern. Tell us what had happened earlier that evening."

Ricord's eyes flickered between Talabot and Graize, who now sat on a chair below the box. "The woman arrived first."

"Mademoiselle Pâquerette?"

He nodded, brusquely. "I let her into the room. She asked for a bottle of wine and two glasses. I brought them to her. She told me to let a gentleman in to see her when he arrived. I went back to the bar."

"And a gentleman did arrive? Mr Blake?"

"Yes. Ten or fifteen minutes later."

"And you let him into the private room? Mademoiselle Pâquerette was still waiting for him?"

"Yes."

"Did you hear any of their conversation?"

"Me? No!" He paused. "Well, I heard her say 'Franklin' when he stepped through the door, and 'you did well to come to see me tonight'. But then they closed the door."

"And how long was it until Inspector Graize came to the tavern, and broke into the room?"

"About an hour."

"And you were in the main part of the tavern all that time?"

235

"Yes."

"No-one else went into the room?"

"No."

"I must ask you about Émile Leboeuf." Ricord shifted uneasily on his feet. "Did Leboeuf have a set of tavern-keys, including a key for the back-door to the private room?"

"He was the serving-man, of course he did." There was an acid tone to Ricord's voice.

Talabot's voice betrayed momentary irritation. "I am simply seeking to establish the facts, Monsieur Ricord. Since Leboeuf had a key, have you any reason to think that he might have entered the room that evening when Mr Blake and Mademoiselle Pâquerette had their meeting?"

"Émile wasn't working that evening. He went to a political rally."

"Thank you. So no-one else could have been in that room." Talabot took a few seconds to look round the court. "Finally, Monsieur Ricord, were Mr Blake and Mademoiselle Pâquerette known to you already, before they came to your tavern last week?"

"Yes."

"Please explain how."

236

"They used to come to the *Auberge des Dunes* five years ago. For a few weeks, they couldn't get enough of each other. Then the Englishman suddenly disappeared, and left his little actress high and dry."

"So Mr Blake abandoned Mademoiselle Pâquerette after a *liaison* that lasted several weeks. Well, they say in English that hell hath no fury like a woman scorned. It is clear that Suzanne Pâquerette had not forgotten her humiliation, and that, when she confronted Mr Blake five years later, his response was to make their separation even more final, by taking her life." With a final authoritative look around the court, Talabot sat down.

"Monsieur Ricord," Denonvilliers began. "You have said that you remembered Mr Blake from five years ago. Was your memory of him a positive one?"

The landlord shifted slightly where he stood. "He was a former customer. What more can I say?"

"What more indeed?" the lawyer repeated. "Well, you could for example explain to the court that you loaned Mr Blake a large sum of money when he was last in Paris, and that you sent a representative to England a year after he departed to ensure that the money was repaid. Is that not the case?" Ricord nodded, begrudgingly. "Answer yes if that is the case, Monsieur Ricord."

"Yes."

"So your feelings towards Mr Blake may not have been very friendly?"

Ricord shrugged. "I got my money back."

"You have also said that your tavern had not been in trouble with the law before. Can you tell us, therefore, if you were surprised that Inspector Graize came to the *Auberge des Dunes* that evening, before the attack on Mademoiselle Pâquerette was discovered?"

The landlord's eyes darted to and fro. "No."

"No, you can't tell us -- or no, you weren't surprised?"

"I wasn't surprised."

"And why were you not surprised, Monsieur Ricord?"

"It's his *quartier*. He looks in on all the taverns from time to time."

"So he is a regular visitor to the *Auberge des Dunes*?"

"You could say so."

Denonvilliers paused. "Émile Leboeuf." Ricord's face darkened. "How long had he worked for you?"

"Long enough." There was an undertone of contempt in the reply.

"I would ask you to be more precise, Monsieur Ricord. One year, two years?"

"Three or four months. I took him on at the start of the summer."

"And were you happy with him?"

Ricord took his time. "He did his job."

"And his job included moving barrels and other supplies into the storage space behind the private room?"

"Yes."

"And he had keys to all the doors, including the one between that space and the private room?"

"Yes."

"Monsieur Ricord, we have heard from Inspector Graize that Émile Leboeuf died yesterday, when he was being arrested for the murder of Louis Rougemont. I understand that that murder took place only two days after Monsieur Rougemont had a meeting in the same private room in your tavern, and that Leboeuf may have eavesdropped on that meeting."

"I knew nothing about that." Ricord said sourly.

Denonvilliers gave him a long look. "I am not suggesting that you did. But I ask you this - if you knew nothing about the fact that Leboeuf eavesdropped on Louis Rougemont's meeting, is it not possible that Leboeuf was in the storage area last Wednesday

239

evening and that he entered the private room and ended the life of Suzanne Pâquerette -- and that you knew nothing about that either?" The lawyer's voice had grown steadily louder, and his last question resonated around the court-room, stirring a new clamour among the spectators. Graize, who had listened closely to the landlord's evidence, was now flushed with anger; it was as much as he could do to remain seated. Ricord seemed unable to find an answer. When the noise had died down again, Denonvilliers repeated his question.

"That cannot have happened," Ricord finally replied. "Leboeuf left the tavern earlier that evening to go to a rally. I said that before. I saw him leave."

"But did you look in the storage area after he left, and before Mr Blake and Mademoiselle Pâquerette had their meeting? Can you be sure that Leboeuf did not come back?" Ricord had no more to say. Now it was Denonvilliers' turn to stand silently and then sit down.

Talabot at once stood up again. "Monsieur le Président, I have one more question to put to this witness. Monsieur Ricord, I understand that Émile Leboeuf was suspected of murdering Louis Rougemont to steal money from him. Was any money taken from Suzanne Pâquerette or Franklin Blake that evening?"

It took Ricord some seconds to grasp what he was being asked. "No. Blake's wallet had fallen to the floor, but was untouched. As for the woman, her purse was still with her."

"Thank you." He addressed the presiding judge. "I have no more witnesses to call. I trust that the court will share my view that the evidence given by Inspector Graize and Monsieur Ricord allows no doubt as to identity of the murderer of Suzanne Pâquerette. Franklin Blake had every reason to wish her dead and, when the opportunity presented itself last Wednesday, he took it and put her to death."

The judge nodded to Talabot, and then turned to the defending lawyer. "Maître Denonvilliers, you have indicated that you wish to call additional witnesses."

Denonvilliers stood up. "Thank you. I should like the court to hear from two other witnesses. The first is Police Captain Lucien de Boizillac; the second is Monsieur Charles Rasquin. Both are present in the court-room."

Talabot was on his feet again. "Monsieur le Président, before these witnesses are called, may I request an adjournment of proceedings?"

"For what reason?"

"Your Honour, I am embarrassed to admit that I have documents relevant to the evidence that Messieurs de Boizillac and Rasquin may give, but I appear to have left them in my *bureau*."

"I am surprised by your oversight, Maître Talabot." The presiding judge conferred briefly with his colleagues at either side of him. "Very well, we will agree an hour's adjournment, no longer." The judges stood up and left the court-room through a door behind their chairs.

Chapter Fourteen

Friday 24 September 1852 - Paris - Rue de Grenelle 103

Ferdinand Talabot needed an adjournment not to recover missing papers, but so that he could pen the message which was delivered urgently to Victor de Persigny:

"Denonvilliers intends to question both Boizillac and Rasquin in court. Boizillac may be no problem; Rasquin is almost certain to be. If you have any power to intervene before Rasquin makes a fool of himself, you may wish to do so. FT"

Persigny stood in his Ministerial office, reading the hastily written note. Ah, Rasquin! He shook his head, despairingly. He felt a loyalty to the man, but he was under no illusions about him. If Rasquin was called into the witness-box, all manner of indiscretions could result. It was not to be contemplated.

Talabot's message precipitated a decision which Persigny had been turning over in his mind since the start of the day, when Morny had unexpectedly appeared in his office. Their conversation had been brief, but forceful. Of course, Persigny knew all about the Prince-President's earlier association with Suzanne Pâquerette, but he had been happy to believe that any threat to his political master had died with her. The letter which Morny brought shattered that belief: Graize had told him that he had seized any incriminating correspondence, but at least one letter survived, and there could be more; and Boizillac knew about the *liaison*, and perhaps others did as well. Even Rasquin?

It was Persigny's turn to put pen to paper. It took him only a minute or two to write his letter, place it in an envelope and close it with his Ministerial seal. He rang the bell for his private secretary, and handed him the letter. "See to it that this reaches the Palais de Justice and is in the hands of Judge de Lavalette within the next half-hour." Persigny's face showed the distaste he felt at what he had done; he grimaced to think that Morny would feel vindicated; but if his action served the Imperial cause, he would have no second thoughts.

***

Friday 24 September 1852 - Paris - Palais de Justice

The hour had passed. The three judges returned to their seats. Aristide de Lavalette addressed the court. "We shall resume. Maître Talabot, I trust that you can now proceed. Maître Denonvilliers, you wish to call additional witnesses."

But the prosecuting attorney was first to his feet. "Monsieur le Président, I have the documents that I need. However, if the court felt able to allow a little longer --"

244

"It does not." The presiding judge's reply was short and to the point. "There has been enough delay.   Maître Denonvilliers."

"I call Captain Lucien de Boizillac." All eyes turned on the young man as he entered the witness-box: none watched him more closely than Alfred Graize. "Captain de Boizillac, you were also in the *Auberge des Dunes* in the evening of last Wednesday. What was the reason for your visit?"

"I was trying to track down an individual - one Jacques Cotte - who had escaped arrest a few days before, not far from the Rue de Calais. I wanted to speak to Inspector Graize in case he had heard anything about Cotte. I happened to see him in the tavern and went in."

"And that was just before Inspector Graize broke down the door to the private room?"

"Yes."

"What did you see in that room?"

"Only what Inspector Graize has already described. The woman, Suzanne Pâquerette, lay dead on the floor. Mr Blake lay on top of her, unconscious."

"Did you assist further in examining the scene of the crime?"

"No." Boizillac paused. "Inspector Graize did not want my assistance."

"So you left the *Auberge des Dunes* again quite soon. What did you do then?"

"I saw someone leaving the tavern in a hurry. I followed and got into the carriage that he had summoned. It was Louis Rougemont."

"Mr Blake's host in Paris? And you accompanied him to his home?"

"In the Rue Marbeuf, yes."

"And did you learn anything more about the circumstances in which Mr Blake had gone to the tavern to meet Mademoiselle Pâquerette?"

"Only what has already been said, that she had contacted him and wanted to confront him about their former *liaison*. That is all I learnt from Louis Rougemont."

"But you subsequently discovered more from his man-servant?"

"I went to the Rue Marbeuf again on Monday of this week, after Rougemont was found dead in the canal. His man-servant told me that a third party - a Monsieur L - had rented the house for Rougemont and had given him instructions on acting as host to Mr Blake and his wife."

"Do you know who this Monsieur L is?"

Boizillac shook his head. "No. But I did receive a letter from him, on Tuesday, in which he wrote that the invitation from Rougemont to Mr Blake to visit Paris had been part of a plan to bring disgrace on Mr Blake, instigated by an English client of Monsieur L. And he also wrote that Louis Rougemont had gone back to the *Auberge des Dunes* two days after the murder, and had seen that Émile Leboeuf had his own keys to the doors leading into the private room." Boizillac looked across at the other policeman. "I was able to communicate this fact to Inspector Graize, and it was this information that led to the decision to arrest Leboeuf."

"Well, we have already heard about that attempted arrest and the consequences," Denonvilliers said. "But, to return to the meeting between Mr Blake and Mademoiselle Pâquerette -- are we to understand that this came about not because Suzanne Pâquerette happened to recognise Mr Blake last week, but because it had been planned some time earlier as part of this effort to discredit him?"

"That is my understanding, based on the letter I received from Monsieur L."

"And do you think that it may be possible that Mademoiselle's intention to invite Mr Blake to the *Auberge des Dunes* that evening was known about in advance by others, not just by Monsieur L and, we must assume, Monsieur Rougemont? If so, who else might have had that knowledge?"

It was a question that Boizillac had turned over in his own mind. But, even as he prepared to answer, proceedings were interrupted as an usher stepped through the door behind the judges and placed an envelope in the hands of Aristide de Lavalette. The presiding judge cut across the examination. "Maître Denonvilliers, I must ask you and the witness to pause for a few moments while I read this communication."

Denonvilliers nodded his acknowledgement, while Boizillac and everyone else in the court-room looked towards the judicial bench. Anyone who had studied Talabot's face would have noticed that the prosecuting attorney was particularly attentive.

De Lavalette broke the envelope open, read the enclosed letter, then passed it to both his colleagues in turn and conferred with them in a low voice. Their heads moved in agreement. De Lavalette addressed the court. "Maître Denonvilliers, the witness should stand down." There was no arguing with the tone of his voice; Boizillac left the box and returned to his seat. "I have now to address your client. Mr Franklin Blake, you will stand up." Blake looked uncomprehendingly at his lawyer, who gestured to him to get to his feet. He did so.

De Lavalette lifted up the document with his right hand. "Mr Blake, I have just received this communication from His Excellency Vicomte de Persigny, Minister of the Interior, written earlier this morning. I shall read it to the court. *'By the authority vested in me by the Prince-President, Louis-Napoléon Bonaparte, I hereby direct that Mr Franklin Blake is to be released from the*

248

custody of the court and allowed to return to his native country of England; and that, without prejudice to the determination of culpability for the murder of Suzanne Pâquerette, the judicial proceedings against Mr Blake are to be stayed and suspended, and Mr Blake shall not be subject to such proceedings either now or in the future.' "

His reading had been heard in complete silence. De Lavalette spoke again. "You are free to leave, Mr Blake. This trial has concluded." A wave of noise suddenly broke from the spectators above and washed through the room. It seemed to shock Franklin Blake into the realisation that his ordeal had ended. With tears in his eyes, he looked up to find his wife. Seeing her, he smiled broadly, then fell back on to his chair.

Denonvilliers struggled to make himself heard. "This is an unexpected, but welcome, development, Monsieur le Président. But do I understand that Mr Blake's release is without prejudice to deciding the question of who was guilty for Mademoiselle Pâquerette's murder? In other words, Mr Blake is a free man, but he has not been exonerated of suspicion for that murder?"

"You have heard the terms which His Excellency the Minister of the Interior has specified for your client's release. Do you wish to challenge them?"

Denonvilliers raised his hands to dismiss the notion. "By no means. We welcome the intervention of His Excellency, and I am sure that my client will be very happy to return to England as soon as possible. I wish only to make it clear that Mr Blake firmly denies any responsibility for the untimely death of Mademoiselle Pâquerette."

"So be it. I repeat, the trial is concluded. Let the court-room be cleared." De Lavalette's voice was all but lost in the hubbub. He and his fellow judges left their seats and the room; their departure prompted a general exodus of lawyers, witnesses and spectators, all speculating loudly on what they had just seen and heard. There was a grim smile on Talabot's face as he nodded towards Graize and strode quickly from the room; but there was thunder in the police inspector's eyes, an unconcealed anger that, against expectation, the Englishman had escaped conviction.

Denonvilliers waited for the court-room to empty completely before guiding Blake out and into the corridor. Some twenty paces away stood Matthew Bruff, and Rachel Blake. The two lawyers held back as husband and wife walked to meet each other. They embraced for a long time.

Bruff came to shake the hand of the French advocate. "Thank you, Antoine." Despite his best efforts, there was a tear in the eye of the English lawyer. "Thank you for all you have done for my dear Rachel, and for Franklin."

Denonvilliers raised his hands as if in protest. "I am pleased to see them reunited. But perhaps we should be thanking His Excellency the Minister of the Interior, though I think that he was motivated not by a sense of clemency, but by a wish to avoid political embarrassment." He shrugged. "Tell me, Matthew,

Captain de Boizillac spoke of this plan to disgrace Mr Blake, which was initiated by a fellow Englishman. Do you know any more? And will you be pursuing the matter further?"

"That remains to be seen," Bruff replied, his good mood momentarily troubled by the thought of the plan. "I told Rachel, Mrs Blake, what I knew, but her only concern has been to see her husband emerge from this trial. She has no interest in seeking revenge for past wrongs."

"A remarkable young woman. Ah, I see that they are approaching us."

His left arm threaded through the right arm of his wife, Blake was transformed. He stood tall, and smiled broadly as he spoke: "My most estimable Bruff, and Maître Denonvilliers, I am indebted to both of you."

"What will you do now?" the French lawyer asked.

"Return to England as soon as we possibly can!"

"We shall be back in London by tomorrow," Rachel said. "And then we shall travel on to our house in Yorkshire. We shall do better to avoid society for the moment."

"And I shall see dear old Betteredge again. What a story I'll have to tell him." Blake's eyes sparkled now.

"Well, then," Rachel said. "You must forgive us, Monsieur Denonvilliers, if we wish to leave Paris with all possible speed. You have been a good friend to us, but too many others in this city have treated us with ill-will and trickery. We shall go to our hotel and make ready for our departure."

Denonvilliers bowed his head to her, in farewell, and shook hands first with Blake, and then with Bruff. The three of them left the Palais de Justice, watched thoughtfully by the French lawyer.

Chapter Fifteen
Tuesday 28 September 1852 - Paris - Rue de Calais

It was an hour after nightfall. It was raining, again. Boizillac had his coat-collar turned up against the weather. The irony of the situation was not lost on him. Two weeks before he had stepped into the *Auberge des Dunes* in order to ask Graize if he knew anything about Jacques Cotte, the anti-Bonapartist who had escaped arrest. Now he was returning to the tavern, but in response to a curt letter that the police inspector had sent him earlier that day: "*Come to the Auberge des Dunes at 9 tonight if you want to find out about Cotte.*" Boizillac showed the letter to Delourcq, and they agreed that this was a meeting that he would keep on his own.

He was only twenty paces away from the tavern when he realised that it was dark and silent - shutters had been closed over the windows, and there was no sign of anyone drinking inside. He tried the handle of the door on to the street. It was locked. Then he heard a key turn and the door opened.

Graize stood inside, with a burning candle in his hand. "Come in," he barked.

Boizillac did so. The door was locked again behind him. There was no light apart from the candle, but that was enough to see that the place was deserted. "What has happened here?"

"Ricord threw in the towel," the inspector growled. "It was bad enough that the woman was murdered. But when it turned out that Leboeuf was a killer, Ricord saw no hope for the place. He closed it down and wants to sell it off."

"But he's not here now? How are you able to use the place?"

Graize paused, then said darkly: "Ricord and I have an understanding."

Boizillac noted the admission, but chose not to dwell on it. "You have information about Jacques Cotte?"

"More than that," was the reply. "I have Cotte himself, and I intend to hand him over to you."

Boizillac could not hide the surprise in his voice. "You have Cotte? Where?"

"We'll come to that. But first let's talk about the murder of Suzanne Pâquerette." He gestured towards one of the tables. Boizillac sat down, increasingly puzzled by the way the meeting was going. Graize took one of the other chairs. "You involved yourself in the investigation almost as much as I did." The younger man made as if to protest. "Spare me your explanations. Just say what you think happened."

They looked at each other in the darkened room for a few seconds, then Boizillac spoke. "I don't believe that Blake killed her. Either he drank too much, or he was drugged, the killing was done, and he was placed on top of the woman to incriminate him." Graize said nothing, but the candle-light showed a fierce glint in his eyes. "We know that there was access to that room from the storage area. I believe that the killer was hiding in that area when Blake and Suzanne Pâquerette met. When the time came - that is, when Blake was inebriated - the killer came out, strangled the woman, and left Blake lying on her." Again, there was no response. "And I have very little doubt that the killer was Leboeuf."

Graize leaned forward. "But why would Leboeuf kill the woman?"

"Perhaps because that was the nature of the man - he killed Rougemont, didn't he?" Boizillac took his time before continuing. "Or perhaps because he had been told to kill her."

"Told? By whom?" he barked.

"Ricord?"

"And why would Ricord tell him to do that?"

Boizillac paused again. "Because Suzanne Pâquerette had another former liaison that she was threatening to reveal, a liaison with a man far more powerful than Blake. And because one of that man's agents had instructed Ricord to arrange for Suzanne Pâquerette to be dealt with."

The conversation stopped. As the seconds went by, the silence in the tavern seemed to grow heavier and to press down on the two men more and more forcefully. Suddenly Graize stood up, went to check that the key in the street-door held it locked, then turned to face Boizillac again. "I should respect you, Boizillac. I should respect your persistence and your commitment to getting at the truth." He gave a snort of contempt. "But I am disgusted by it - look at what it has achieved! A trial that would have ended satisfactorily has been abandoned, and no-one has been found guilty of the murder of the actress."

"Yet you know that Blake wasn't guilty, don't you? And you know that Suzanne Pâquerette's death was part of a conspiracy, involving Leboeuf, Ricord -- and others."

Graize walked across to stand directly above Boizillac, then he leaned forward to say: "Yes, I know all that, Boizillac. I know it because I serve this regime and am trusted by it. Would that the same could be said of you."

Boizillac waited until the other man retreated. "Then let me ask you one question, Graize, which has been in my mind for the last few days. Did Ricord tell you in advance that there was a plan for Mademoiselle Pâquerette to confront Blake here, that night? And did you then instruct him to exploit that meeting, to serve the regime?"

"I was sure that you would reach that conclusion."

"And am I right?"

Graize's only answer was a short laugh. Then he commanded: "Follow me." He gestured for Boizillac to get up, went to the internal door to the private room and unlocked it. "Here's Cotte."

The room was weakly illuminated by a candle in a holder on the table. On a chair next to it sat a gagged figure. Boizillac could see that the man's hands and feet were bound together, and that he was lashed to the chair by a rope that looped twice around his torso and was drawn tight by a knot at the chair-back. He could see as well that the man's face was badly bruised, and that blood was leaking through his shirt where the rope bit into him. He was watching the two police agents closely.

"How did you find him?"

"This is my *quartier*. I know all the hiding-places."

"And you're handing him over to me?"

Graize gave no reply, but reached inside his coat. He took out his pistol, which he placed on the table, and then a long-bladed knife. He cut through the rope tying Cotte to the chair and undid his feet. "I'll unlock the street-door."

257

He turned to leave the room. Boizillac moved towards the captive. But at that moment Cotte jumped up; even though his wrists were still bound together, he seized the pistol and raised it in the air. There was a flash as he pulled the trigger. Boizillac was momentarily blinded. He heard a loud thud from the bar area, and felt Cotte push past him. And then he saw the body of Graize on the floor; his head had been shattered by the bullet; his limbs shook for a few seconds; then he was dead.

Cotte was by the street-door. He managed to rip the gag from his mouth. "Listen to me, and don't try to stop me. That bastard," he gestured with the pistol at Graize, "when he'd finished beating my face to a pulp, told me to play along with his game, and then I'd go free. He told me you'd come here tonight. I was supposed to wait in that room until he untied me. Then I'd pick up his pistol and shoot you. Yes, you." Cotte spat in the direction of the dead man. "I thought about it. But I could see through his plan. Let me go? Never! So I decided to do for the lying bastard.

"I've done you a favour, see? So now I'm going to open this door and disappear. Don't try to stop me, or it'll be the worse for you. Got it?" Without waiting for an answer, Cotte unlocked the door and was gone into the rain.

Boizillac stood unmoving for some seconds. He was letting Cotte escape for a second time -- a man who opposed the regime, and who had just shot dead one of the leading agents of the Paris police. But Boizillac didn't doubt that Cotte had spoken true. Graize had brought him to the tavern and confirmed Boizillac's assumptions about Suzanne Pâquerette's death because he planned for the younger man to be killed. He stared at the corpse at his feet.

Delourcq came rushing into the tavern. "Captain, are you in here?" He saw Boizillac, and then the lifeless form of Graize. "Sweet Jesus!"

"Delourcq? Why are you here?"

"I decided to keep an eye on you, from a distance. I was outside, round the corner. I heard gunshot and stumbled round on these old legs, and saw someone running away."

"That was Jacques Cotte. He shot Graize dead in front of me."

Boizillac slumped on to a chair. Delourcq looked behind the bar, found a third-full bottle of cognac and two glasses, and poured measures for both of them. "Drink this, captain. We've lost Cotte, and we don't need to hurry to deal with Graize." He took a mouthful. "When you've had a drop or two, you can tell me what happened."

The bottle was empty when they left an hour later. Delourcq had rooted out an old table-cloth to cover the dead man. Boizillac locked the tavern behind them. They would return in the morning. Before then, they both had their women to go to.

Wednesday 29 September 1852 - Paris - Rue de Grenelle 103

Persigny studied the report that Boizillac had written about the latest killing in the *Auberge des Dunes*. Well, Graize had served him well, but he had over-reached himself, and Persigny's regrets at the loss of one of his agents was tempered by the thought that with his death the man had taken with him so much knowledge of the secret workings of the regime. There would be others to take his place.

Persigny went to the cabinet in the corner of the room. With care, he fetched out the bee pendant that Rasquin had brought him, and allowed candle-light to play on its shining surfaces. Never mind the price paid, in money or in lives, this was a powerful talisman for the return of the Empire. And that must happen soon now.

***

Friday 1 October 1852 - London - Bethnal Green Cut

Octavius Luker sat in his office.

It was a week since he had returned from Paris. He had stayed there, *incognito*, to watch the trial, and he had seen at first hand how the prosecution of Franklin Blake had been terminated.

Ablewhite *père* came to see him once more, and for the last time, on Monday. Shorter of breath than ever when he had climbed the stairs and dropped into an armchair, his first words were: "Well done, Luker. The Frenchies let him go. The two of them were back here on Saturday and they've gone straight up to Yorkshire." He paused, mopped his brow, then continued. "My wife has been shedding tears of joy enough to float a battle-ship."

"I am pleased to hear it," Luker said quietly.

"This has been a lesson to me, I don't mind admitting. I don't doubt that it's taken Mr Franklin Blake down a peg or two -- but if I'd have known how it would turn out, I would never have started down this road."

"If I may add something, sir, you were not to know that there would be others on that road who had their own plans for Mr Blake, and Mademoiselle Pâquerette."

His client shot Luker a glance. "I thank you for that, but it won't answer. I started this ball rolling, and I bear responsibility for the damage done." He breathed deeply. "I shall have to admit my part in this -- in due course, at any rate. It's too soon at the moment." He took an envelope from his coat-pocket and placed it on Luker's table. "I have much reason to thank you, Luker. I give you this in full and final payment for your services. I don't expect to call on you again." He got to his feet. "I think that this concludes our business."

"Might I ask one last thing?" Luker said. "For myself, I feel particular regret over the death of Louis Rougemont. You may recall that he had a French father and an English mother. I learnt that Lucinda Rougemont, née Peverill, died some twenty years ago, and that her body was brought back to be buried in this country. Her remains lie in a churchyard in Chislehurst. I cannot arrange for Louis Rougemont's body to be transferred to this country, but, with your concurrence, sir, I should like to go to Chislehurst and seek the agreement of the priest to place a stone commemorating the young man in the churchyard, near his mother's grave."

There was a brief silence. Then: "You have my blessing, Luker. And if you need money from me to achieve this, let me know. I won't be found wanting." He left.

That had been four days earlier. Now Luker had just received and read a letter from Guillaume. He had completed shutting down the house in the Rue Marbeuf; as a postscript he added that there had been one more killing in the tavern in the Rue des Dunes, of Inspector Graize.

So, after Suzanne Pâquerette and Louis Rougemont, Alfred Graize's life had also been ended by violence. He thought back over the past year, and recalled especially his conversations with Graize, for he had been the Paris police's representative at the Great Exhibition, and he had given Luker information about the *Auberge des Dunes* and its landlord. Only Ricord had escaped what seemed like the fatal curse striking at those he'd involved in the plan to disgrace Franklin Blake. Luker wondered whether even Ricord would remain unscathed.

The investigation agent pulled on his coat, and went out to take the train to Chislehurst.

NOTE ON CHARACTERS

Historical characters

Louis-Napoléon Bonaparte was born in 1808, the son
of Louis Bonaparte, younger brother of Napoléon
Bonaparte, and Hortense de Beauharnais. After the
Battle of Waterloo and the collapse of the First Empire
in 1815, Louis-Napoléon lived mainly in exile until
1848. That year saw the end of the Orleanist monarchy
in France, the creation of the Second Republic, and the
election of a President by universal suffrage.   Louis-
Napoléon, who had returned to France, won that
election with almost three-quarters of the votes cast.
His term of office was limited to four years, but in
December 1851 he staged a *coup d'état* to seize full
control of the country, and to prepare the way for the
replacement of the Republic in December 1852 by the
inauguration of a Second Empire. This was to last until
1870, when defeat in the Franco-Prussian War saw
Louis-Napoléon exiled again and the creation of a Third
Republic. He died in 1873.

Charles de Morny was born in 1811, the son of an
adulterous union between Charles de Flahaut and
Hortense de Beauharnais: this meant that he was the
half-brother of Louis-Napoléon. After serving in the

Army and making a career in French business and political circles for more than decade, he became one of his half-brothers closest advisers and co-conspirator in the 1851 *coup d'état*. His reward was to be appointed Minister of the Interior for the new regime, though he gave up this position in early 1852 in order to return to business. He died in 1865.

Victor de Persigny was born in 1808, under the name of Jean-Gilbert-Victor Fialin. A life-long supporter of Louis-Napoléon, even during his years in exile, he was also among the small group of conspirators who implemented the *coup* in December 1851. He replaced Morny as Interior Minister in 1852, and used his ministerial powers to prepare the way for the announcement of the Second Empire at the end of that year. He died in 1872.

Other characters

Lucien de Boizillac was born in 1820 and raised as the son of Alexandre and Madeleine de Boizillac. Only three decades later did he discover that his natural parents were Madeleine's sister, Geneviève de Lassource, and Charles de Flahaut. After serving in the Army until 1849, he became a captain in the Paris police. His role in investigating murders committed in the weeks preceding Louis-Napoléon's seizure of power in December 1851 is described in the novel "Coup de Tête".

Franklin Blake was born in 1823, the son of a rich but eccentric father who sent him abroad, to Germany,

France and Italy, for most of his formative years. He returned to England only in 1848 to celebrate the 18th birthday of his cousin, *Rachel Verinder*. An alliance between the two cousins was initially prevented by the theft from Rachel's house of a precious jewel, but after a year's separation the two married by the end of 1849. The story of Franklin Blake, Rachel Verinder and the jewel itself is told in the novel "The Moonstone", by Wilkie Collins (published in 1868).

Octavius Luker was born in 1811, to a family poor in money but rich in progeny. After trying his hand at different occupations, Luker discovered that his talents were best suited to private investigation work. His brother, Septimus Luker, a money-lender, appears in "The Moonstone"; Octavius Luker does not.

In memory of Jeremy Michael Cresswell
1949 to 2015

Also by Paul Bristow

"COUP DE TÊTE"

Paris. November 1851.

This is not the city of lights that became celebrated under the Second Empire, but a maze of narrow streets clogged with filth, and rank with disease, poverty and crime.

Three years after its birth, the Second Republic is a sickly child, with few friends, many enemies, and an elected President who is the nephew of Napoleon I and who makes no secret of his wish to bring back the imperial rule of his uncle.

A corpse is found in the cess-pits of Montfaucon - stripped, murdered and decapitated. This first grisly crime foreshadows more to come.

Solving the murder falls to Captain Lucien de Boizillac, of the Sûreté division of the Paris Police. Boizillac, at the age of thirty, retains the attachment to the myth of Napoleonic glory which he acquired during his years in the French army of occupation in Algeria.

As his partner in the investigation of the murder, the Sûreté assigns Daniel Delourcq, an old Parisian lag turned enforcement agent, who lacks the younger man's elegance, but matches his energy with hard-won experience and cunning.

The murders and mutilations continue. In time Boizillac and Delourcq discover whose hand has been wielding the knife, and who stands in the shadows behind the killer, directing the butchery. As political developments rush towards a violent resolution, Boizillac seeks to confront the instigator of the killings, and is himself confronted with a dilemma, setting his sense of duty against family and political loyalties.

When the *coup d'état* comes on 2 December 1851, it is a blow not only against the French constitution but also against the structure of Boizillac's own cherished beliefs.

(published by YouWriteOn.com, 2011)

Lightning Source UK Ltd.
Milton Keynes UK
UKOW03f1053020517

300311UK00001B/27/P